To my parents.
Because everything.

AHMED AZIZ'S

EPIC

YEAR

NINA HAMZA

Quill Tree Books
An Imprint of HarperCollinsPublishers

BOOK
ONE

CHAPTER
ONE

Three years ago, we moved for the first time in my life. In fact, apart from the two nights at a neighbor's house when half the town was looking for my dad, I had spent every night of my twelve years in the same house, sleeping in the same room, in the same bed.

Three years ago, I learned that sometimes you have choices without having a choice. Like getting to eat out, as long as it's an Indian restaurant. Or buying a new video game, as long as it's "parent approved." Or choosing something new to wear for Eid, as long as it's fancy.

Three years ago, we had to leave Hawaii. We had no choice. We could have moved to California, or Japan, or Minnesota. We had choices.

My parents chose Minnesota.

Story of my life.

CHAPTER
TWO

I was mad at Mom for making us move our lives while Dad was still sick. *Seething.* No conversations, no discussions.

I pulled a guava off the tree before getting in the car. The tree Dad had planted the day I was born, with a line scratched and a date carved on the trunk marking my height on every birthday. I slouched down, arms crossed, and baseball hat pulled low. I waited for Mom to notice how angry I was. I watched her out of the corner of my eye, tapping on the steering wheel, bobbing her head from side to side, and singing all the wrong words to a Prince song. "Gimme a red Corvette. Baby, you're much too bad." The guava was hard and still sour. Sara joined in from the back, clapping and snapping out of tune and out of sync. I was surrounded by weirdos.

"Come on, Ahmed!" Mom yelled over the music,

either oblivious or unaffected by my anger. I looked out the window instead.

I hated visiting hours. Don't get me wrong, I love my dad. I especially love my memories of Dad before he got sick. What I didn't love was the unpredictability. If his hair was unbrushed and the blinds were closed, it was going to be a rough visit. Sometimes he barely recognized me. If he was showered and sunshine flooded the room, he would be ready to come home.

Sara climbed between the front seats to get out of the car, stepping on my fingers, adding injury to insult. Maybe a move to Minnesota would mean a car with back doors that opened.

I made my guesses as we waited for the elevator. The family with the balloons was obviously a sixth-floor family. They were laughing, and the little girl wore a pink *I'm a big sister now* T-shirt. They were going to the labor and delivery floor. The man with the gray beard and bald head who didn't look up when the girl started to sing must have been an eighth-floor family. That was the cancer floor.

The seventh floor was ours. Squeezed between the joy of new babies and the sadness of cancer, the seventh floor was where my father had spent too many months of the past year.

Cirrhosis, the doctor called it, his lisp stinging my ears

like static on the radio. A year ago, Dad's doctor drew pictures on the whiteboard explaining how a backed-up liver let toxins build up until Dad became confused and goofy. He called it a blocked drain, like bad plumbing. Bad plumbing makes your toilets overflow; it doesn't make your dad forget who you are. I asked the doctor why Dad's liver was cirrhotic. Was it something we brought home from school like lice or strep throat? The doctor smiled so wide, his eyes turned to tiny slits. No, he assured us, that's not how cirrhosis works. Dad had a rare genotype of hepatitis C, the doctor explained, but I didn't understand what he meant. Sometimes you can have all the right words but not know how to use them. What they meant to say was that Dad had an infection, a type of hepatitis C, a type he inherited from his mom, a type that was hard to cure. The only solution, they all agreed, was a liver transplant, but *rare genotype* apparently also meant they couldn't give him one.

The seventh floor was also the transplant floor, but my father was an impostor, because he needed a transplant and couldn't get one. So even when the whiteboard cheerfully spelled "Happy Birthday, Bilal!" in multicolored balloon letters, I hated it.

I pushed the door open with my back, my hands gripping the still warm plate of pakodas. The room was bright, and Dad was smiling. It was going to be a good visit.

"What's going on, guys?" he asked. "I'm looking forward to some company today. Missed all of you." The white of his eyes was a lighter yellow than two days ago.

Sara started, not taking a moment to breathe. She filled him in on her latest dance recital and the book she was writing and how she was going to learn to knit scarves and sell them at the fair and how she was going to donate all the money she would make to research for liver disease. She had a hundred plans brewing. Most of them were created on the spot, and none of them would leave the room with her.

Dad focused on scratching his arm, not meeting my eyes. "What about you, Ahmed? Do you hate me?"

Hate him?

"Umm . . . for what?" I asked.

"Well, I'm sure you're not thrilled about moving to Minnesota, but the doctors say that's the place to be. There's an experimental treatment for my hepatitis and an experienced surgeon that may be the perfect combination for me."

"What?" I was confused.

"They think I have a decent chance of getting ready for a liver transplant, and—"

"We're moving to Minnesota because *you* want to?" I asked.

I looked at Mom, but she was helping Sara get gum out of her hair, her back turned to me.

"*Want* is a strong word, Ahmed. This treatment is only available in a few places. Japan, California, and Minnesota."

"And you chose Minnesota?"

Dad worked on undoing a knot on the tie of his gown, still not meeting my eyes. Sometimes, in the hospital, it was like he was the child and I was the grown-up. *Don't scratch your arm*, I wanted to tell him. *Don't play with that knot.*

"Yeah, I didn't think I'd be ready either. I loved Minnesota when I was a child." He pulled at the knot, making it tighter, not looser. "I didn't think I'd ever want to move back, you know, because . . ."

"Because your brother died?" I finished his sentence for him.

"Yes. It's been a long time, but maybe this is the push I need to go back."

And that was our only conversation about the move, but it was the only one we needed.

CHAPTER
THREE

With zero packing experience, I squeezed twelve years of life into cardboard cartons. Things I couldn't have lived without a month ago—the leftover pieces from the gaming PC I built and the tennis shoes with the frayed laces—had to be given away, and all my belongings with their irregular shapes and curves were squared into eighteen-inch boxes.

It felt like the minute Dad was strong enough to leave the hospital, we were elbowing each other for armrests, eating pretzels, and flying over the Pacific Ocean. Like we couldn't wait to get to Minnesota.

The low battery alert blinked in the corner of my screen, and I searched every pocket of my backpack for my charger.

"Mom, you didn't remind me to pack my charger for the plane."

She ignored my accusation and put a book in my lap instead. For Mom, every situation was an opportunity to shove a book in my lap. She didn't give up easily.

The title was printed across the cover in big red letters. *Holes.* An envelope stuck out in the middle like a thick bookmark. As if I'd ever get halfway through a book. The return address was Cedar Valley Middle School, Farthing, Minnesota. My new school. The envelope had already been opened, and I unfolded the letter inside.

> *Dear Ahmed,*
>
> *I hope you had another wonderful school year. I am excited to have you join us for the sixth-grade accelerated Language Arts class.*
>
> *We have a lot to get through this year.*
>
> *I do have a favor to ask. Could you please read the following books before the first day of school? There's a good chance you've read one, if not all of them, when you were younger. I'd like you to read them again. We are going to study the stories in these books and learn how they are still relevant to our lives. We will study what we like in them and discuss what we don't. My hope is we will learn to find commonality in what first seems distant from our day-to-day existence.*
>
> *At the end of the year I'm always thrilled to hear how*

much everyone has learned when we hold the "Are you smarter than Mrs. Gaarder?" contest, where one group of students uses their knowledge of the books to try to win the huge, shiny, Stanley Cup–sized trophy that has been on my desk for six years. I am yet to be defeated. But there will be brownies.

Happy reading!

Holes *by Louis Sachar*
Bridge to Terabithia *by Katherine Paterson*
From the Mixed-Up Files of Mrs. Basil E. Frankweiler
    by E. L. Konigsburg

Can't wait to meet you!
Mrs. Gaarder

P.S. Ahmed, we're so excited to have you join us in Minnesota. We can't wait to hear all about life in Hawaii and what it's like to catch a wave.

Geez. Was it possible to hate a place before you'd seen it?

I'm not dumb. In fact, quite the opposite. I knew it well before I sat through eight hours of testing in third grade, and before my mom, school counselor, and teachers knew to use phrases like "achieve his potential" and "find his motivation." I think everyone was surprised to discover I'm smart, because I don't read. I mean I know how to do it; I just didn't like to. If you don't like to read, people assume you're dumb. Even more irritating is the idea that if you like to read, you must be smart. I don't like reading, but I like words. I realize that sounds contradictory, but I like how one perfect word can replace a whole sentence. *Efficient.*

I had a better idea for an assignment. I could spend the entire flight studying everything wrong with the letter. For starters, it's wrong to call an assignment a favor. You're not fooling anyone when you do. I hate assumptions. I know what people assume when they think of Hawaii. They assume everyone would be surfing, eating pineapples, or stocking up on Spam. *Stereotypes.* I have never surfed in my life, pineapple makes my mouth itch, and I have never tasted any version of pork, let alone the canned variety.

I already missed the familiarity of what I had, where everyone had known me my entire life, as I had known them. They knew I was a different shade of brown because my parents came from India. They knew we sent biryani to the neighbors on Eid because we were Muslim. They knew Sara would wear tutus every day if

Mom let her. And they knew if the blinds were down in our front window, someone was sick. They knew without needing an explanation.

I had a feeling there would be a lot of explaining in my future.

My finger traced the title, each letter raised so I could follow the word with my eyes closed. *Holes*. Only one word. Which made me like this author better than the others already.

I wondered what kind of holes he was talking about. How many? And what was in them? I'd read enough to find out. But not a page more.

I made it halfway through after all, like the letter wedged in the middle had predicted, and I have to admit it wasn't terrible. Mainly because this Stanley Yelnats was an okay guy. I could see myself hanging out with him. All he wanted was to make a few friends, not worry his parents, and get through being away from home.

I pushed Sara's shoulders back to look out the window as we landed. There was lake after lake, and field after field.

"That's corn and soy," Dad said.

As if I cared. More obvious was what I didn't see. There were no palm trees. There was no beach. And I'll tell you what, for a kid who could count on one hand how many times he'd been to the beach in the last year, I was surprised by how much I missed it.

I thought of that part in *Holes* where Stanley left his home and family. He was on his way to a camp that was more jail and less camp. Looking out the window of the bus, there was nothing but hay and cotton, and he felt like he was on a ride to nowhere.

That's when I recognized it. I liked Stanley so much because he was me. Or maybe I was him.

CHAPTER
FOUR

It was raining when we landed in Minneapolis–
St. Paul ("Twin Cities," Dad said, to uncaring ears),
and our bags took enough time at the conveyor belt to
give strangers the chance to be friendly. "Where're you
kids from?" the old lady holding the carrier with her
dog's head peeking out asked. I hated that question. I
hated having to explain myself with an adjective. I didn't
feel like an Indian American, and it didn't matter that
I had never been to India, because the color of my skin
meant I needed to explain.

"Well, my mom's from India. My dad's parents are
from India, but he's from here. And I'm American." No
adjective, thank you very much.

"That's nice, honey. But I meant where are you flying
from. We're coming in from Seattle. It was raining there
too."

I hate assumptions, even when they're mine. "Oh. We're from Hawaii."

We got drenched waiting for a taxi with our four over-stuffed suitcases, which we shoved and repositioned but couldn't fit in one car. It didn't feel right to get there in two separate cars. Dad and Sara took the first taxi, and Sara spent the ride looking out the back, writing notes to me in big letters pressed against the window, allowing me to ignore my new scenery.

"We're in Minnesota!" Umm, I noticed.

"So exciting!" No way.

"Looks pretty cool." Don't think so.

Our tiny and partially unwilling caravan made its way to our new home. Just like that, we had a new home. Boxes waited patiently for us in a house Mom had picked, in a neighborhood Dad had chosen. We hadn't unlocked the front door before Sara declared it sweet and Mom called it lovely. I thought it was fine. We were in a cul-de-sac; we had a red door; we had a basement. I had never been in a basement, but like every movie, the steps creaked on the way down, and there were corners where no light reached, even with my flashlight. Mom's promise from years ago was finally fulfilled; Sara and I had our own rooms. It was strange to see boxes with my handwriting in a room I had never been. "Computer.

Ahmed's room," I had written in what seemed like a different lifetime, on a different planet. The first time I heard my voice in a video, I was surprised that the words coming out of my mouth sounded nothing like me. This felt the same. I may have written the words, but seeing them in this house made no sense.

I looked around my room. There would never be princesses on the wall or safety pins from half-finished friendship bracelets threatening to poke me on my bed. Instead, there were three dead flies on the floor.

CHAPTER
FIVE

Mom told us stories about her childhood in India any chance she got. When we talked about how the hot dogs at school bounced when you dropped them, she told us about her delicious tiffin box of fried fish and rice. When we complained about no legroom in the backseat, she told us about squeezing fifteen people into an Ambassador car. She'd go on and on. Ad nauseam. Unlike Dad, who said nothing.

"Leave him alone," Mom would say when we pressed him for details. "He's not a sharer."

And he usually wasn't. But every year for his birthday, Dad's friend Janet sent a package from Minnesota, and every Eid aunties and uncles sent cards. The arrival of these pried loose a story or two. Sara and I loved the "opening of the box." We sat on the floor, and Dad ceremoniously sliced through the tape, leaving the top open, colored tissue peeking out. There was always a bag of candy. The red-and-green cover of Nut Goodies, Peppermint Patties, caramels, and taffy. Minnesota candy, Dad called it. Also known as candy available at the gas station around the corner from our house. There was always a brown plastic jug with the label "Maple Syrup Tapped and Packed from Janet's Backyard Just for You" that would make an appearance at our table every Sunday morning for pancakes. A small Ziploc bag stuffed with pressed leaves in red and yellow and gold was Dad's favorite part of the box. He pressed his nose into the bag, taking a long sniff before unwrapping a caramel and leaning back in his chair. Then we'd wait for a story. We chewed on caramels and Dad told us about his trips to pumpkin patches and how he got the scar above his left eyebrow. The year we opened the box in his hospital room, it was over those caramels that he blinked away tears when he spoke about how he missed his brother.

Minnesota Dad was different. It was a continuous opening of the box. We couldn't shut the guy up. From the minute we landed, Dad's phone buzzed with texts and phone calls. With every *Assalamu Alaikum* or *hello*, his voice got louder and his laugh lasted longer. His "maybe this week" turned to "perhaps tonight" and

17

finished with "tonight sounds perfect."

"What's happening tonight?" I asked. We had flown across an ocean, across half the country, and moved into a new house. Wasn't that enough?

Mom pulled the last glasses out of a cardboard box and stacked them in the cupboard. Batman's face on my favorite glass was faded and chipped, making him look angry on the shelf. Me too, buddy.

"People are excited to have your dad back in town. They want us to meet them tonight."

She flattened the box and added it to the growing pile in the corner of the room. Sara stood on the pile and bounced, her only contribution to unpacking.

"They do?" I asked.

There was something comforting about the sound of the box cutter slicing through the top of another box before she emptied and flattened it.

"Well, of course, Ahmed. This is your dad's hometown." She placed another glass in front of Batman, hiding his displeasure. "We call our parents' friends aunty and uncle for a reason. They may not be related by blood, but they're family. And they haven't seen him in over twenty years."

Slice, flatten, pile. Slice, flatten, pile.

Dad joined us in the kitchen and picked up the box

cutter Mom pointed to with a tilt of her head. He lifted a box to the counter. "So it's all set. They've booked a small room at the restaurant down the road for dinner tonight. They want to have a big party for us when I'm done with surgery, but for now they'll make do with dinner." Dad's unpacking didn't have the efficiency of Mom's, and he left a half-empty (or is it half-full?) box on the counter to start a new one.

"Dad," Sara asked, "it doesn't make you sad to be here? Doesn't make you miss your brother?" Leave it to Sara to ask the question I was thinking but didn't have the guts to ask.

He rested his elbows on his open box, still holding a wrapped something. "You know, I thought it would. I left Minnesota the moment I could. But there were so many good things that happened here, too, and right now, that's all I remember." He unwrapped the newspaper protecting a plastic pink cup. A newspaper that would no longer be on the front porch every morning or stacked in the recycling bin every Wednesday neatly tied with brown string. "And besides"—he looked at me and ruffled my hair—"anytime I miss my brother, all I have to do is look at you."

He held the pink cup, unsure where to place it, finally putting it back in the box. "I've said it a million times.

You're the exact copy of my brother. You look like him, talk like him, think like him."

"And he was twelve when he died, wasn't he? Like Ahmed?" Again, Sara put a voice to my thoughts.

Mom dug through the box, found the pink cup, and put it on the shelf. "I'm excited to meet everyone. I've heard so many stories, it's like I know them already." I knew she was trying to change the topic, and I didn't mind.

I wasn't looking forward to dinner. If aunties and uncles in Minnesota were anything like those in Hawaii, there'd be cheek pinching and tight hugging. I had been through enough already.

"Ahmed, try to unpack your clothes before dinner, would you?" Mom asked. "And you too, Sara."

Instead I took my computer apart, looking for what had made it glitch the last few weeks. It felt strange to have all the pieces scattered around the room and not post signs telling Sara to stay away. She chased a squirrel outside my window. I put my computer back together, not finding the problem. Dad called us to leave for dinner. I guess glitches were meant to be a part of my life.

CHAPTER
SIX

We circled the parking lot at the strip mall twice before finding a spot at the opposite end. Wedged between Tony's Pizza and Birds!Birds!Birds! was Taj Mahal restaurant.

"We're meeting at an Indian restaurant? Named Taj Mahal? How original." No one bothered to reply.

"Mom," Sara asked, twirling down the sidewalk before stopping in front of the bird store, "could we buy a birdhouse for our backyard? That would be so cool."

I could smell the restaurant already. Restaurants never smelled like home cooking; it stuck to your hair and got inside your pores. *Pungent.*

"Sure, I think that would be a great idea, Sara," Mom replied. "You two go ahead. We'll be right there."

We opened the door to the Taj Mahal, releasing a big

cheer. There were hugs and tears, and people I had never seen kissed one cheek and then the other and came back for a third. More than once, I went left when they went right, and lips met. I needed mouthwash.

Someone's hip bounced me to the side, knocking me into another poor soul clinging to the walls for safety.

"When I first met the Indian community, as your dad called it, I was overwhelmed too." She held her hand out for me to shake. "I'm Janet, by the way." Janet of maple syrup fame. "Wow," she said, looking right into my eyes, "your dad was right. You look like your uncle." Tapped and packaged just for me.

I was pulled into the crowd before I could reply. For the rest of the evening I was wedged between two over-perfumed aunties, hitting my knee against the table leg, catching hot, buttery naans as they passed by. I didn't see Janet again to thank her for years of maple syrup and Dad stories, but I got my chance eventually.

CHAPTER
SEVEN

I f you are ever forced to move to Minnesota, July is the time to do it.

Mom and Sara suctioned the clear plastic birdhouse they bought to the glass patio door, and soon we had birds, and then squirrels, followed by rabbits looking for anything the others left behind. It felt strange watching the birds so close. *Intrusive.* But they didn't seem to mind. Everyone was outside—on roller blades, bikes, kayaks, walking their dogs, their babies, or themselves. Their time outside felt hectic, unlike the lazy days in Hawaii. I didn't understand it then, but seven months later, in the dead of winter, it would make sense why everyone was rushing to relax.

Dad had his first doctor's appointment. I thought the doctors should have made a bigger deal about it. I mean,

I got a bouncy ball for having my braces tightened, and Dad had moved his entire family for these appointments. That deserved a party, or a medal, or at least a box of chocolate. They gave him three small pills a day for the next few months instead. Three pills that were supposed to try to clear his infection. Three pills that drained his strength.

Somehow *he* still had enough energy to play tour guide for the four of us and *I* was the one yawning. We headed out of Farthing and into "the cities" every day. We took pictures in the sculpture garden, posing in front of the spoon and cherry, rented pedal cars at Minnehaha Park, biked around Lake of the Isles, ate at every food truck we saw, got lost in the skyways, and found the closest halal food market. Mom had only two weeks before she started work, and we made the most of it. We lived like tourists, because according to Dad, once we became locals we'd never see the sights. I had never been a tourist before, and I didn't think I'd ever feel like a local.

We had a blast those first weeks. I think it was their way of apologizing for the move. I'm glad we did, because right after that I met Jack.

Of all the stories Mom repeated, the one we heard most often was about her grandmother, her Ummamma, who lived with them in India when Mom was a child. She was eighty years old and spent most of her day sitting comfortably in the front veranda, in her special chair with long arms that swung forward to become a leg rest. Every morning before school, she'd braid Mom's hair and tell her the story of how her mother had braided *her* hair. Ummamma repeated the story every day using the exact same words, even when she couldn't remember anything else. Whenever we wanted to make sure to remember something, Mom called it a hair-braiding moment. That meant she was trying to tuck that memory into the deepest folds of her brain so she'd never forget. The day we stayed inside during a hurricane warning and watched Harry Potter movies together, or went for a hike where there was no trail and found rocks someone had used to spell out the word *peace*. Those were hair-braiding moments.

I feared meeting Jack would be a hair-braiding moment. But not a moment filled with candy and smiley faces that you talk about with friends on long summer days lying on your back, looking at clouds. It would be the kind of moment you wish you could delete, or at least rewind. And here's the worst part. Not only did Jack go to my school, he also rode my bus. Not only did he ride my bus, he also lived two doors down. That meant, potentially, I could be around Jack 24/7. *Ensnared.*

I met Jack before school started. We met in my garage, where my defenses were down and I wasn't ready.

Boxes we hadn't unpacked yet were stacked in the garage after I persuaded Dad not to put them in the basement. I wasn't excited to go down there every time we needed something. He reminded me that in winter it would be a lot more comfortable searching for something in the warmth of the basement instead of the below freezing of the garage. I'd worry about winter when winter came. Dad's general plan was that if, after a year, it was still in the box, we probably didn't need it and it could be thrown out. Once in a while he'd send me out there to get something for him. He called it search and rescue. As in, could you search and rescue the big pasta pot? Or could you search and rescue the small white trash can? If we needed it, it was rescued. If we didn't, it deserved to be thrown out.

I was on my knees, digging through a big open cardboard box searching for, in an attempt to rescue, the big green ladle, when I heard skateboard wheels on my driveway. It was Jack.

Unlike movies I have watched and books I have been forced to read, you can't tell a bully by looking at him. Maybe that's why I hated books; I never learned anything useful from them. Because Jack looked like a nice guy. With his round face, hair gelled into a wave high enough for a surfer to crouch under, and big blue eyes, he looked like the kind of guy who'd have your back in a fight. I couldn't have been more wrong.

"So, you're the new kid who's going to be in our school?" Two boys hung back while Jack stood on his skateboard, eating a bag of chips, rocking back and forth, trying to stay in one spot.

"Yeah, my name is Ahmed," I replied, and started to get up.

He got off his skateboard and walked toward me, standing so close I smelled Doritos and sweat. The other two didn't come closer, but they also didn't walk away. He turned his chip bag upside down, dumping red crumbs all over my almost-new white tennis shoes. I didn't move. I barely breathed. It was quiet except for the sound of Jack crumpling the empty bag in his hand, and I watched, with my mouth partially open, as he threw it at my chest. "Welcome to Minnesota," he said before riding away on his skateboard. Maybe I could have reacted faster if we weren't in my garage, if I wasn't caught off guard. I doubt it, but maybe.

And I didn't see him again until the first day of school.

CHAPTER
EIGHT

Sara and I were in different schools for the first time. Along with getting lost in a corn maze and gagging on lutefisk, I added it to my running mental list of things I was being forced to experience. Apparently, it was all going to help build my character. I had never been on a school bus before either. In fact, I had never really had a first day of school before. Not the kind of first day where the new kid walks lost in the halls and someone bigger pushes him so papers go flying everywhere. I had never had *that* kind of a first day. I'll admit, I was nervous.

I was so restless all night that when Mom came to wake me, I didn't know if she was there to say good night or good morning. I pulled my favorite shirt over my head, a dark red T-shirt with a silhouette of a surfer on the front and *Hank's Hamburgers* in cursive on the back. The irony of complaining about being associated with surfing and this being my favorite T-shirt was not lost on me. I didn't remember it being so faded or having so many holes in it. I took it off and tried one of the new shirts we had bought for school. I put Hank's Hamburgers back on. Hank, don't fail me now.

It didn't feel like my usual first day of school. The air was lighter, less wet. There were only three of us at our bus stop. Me, a girl who towered over me with a mess of curly black hair and feet to put Michael Jordan to shame, and of course Jack.

In the past few weeks I had seen more farmland than I knew existed. In the middle of flat fields as far as the eye could see rose tall, cylindrical metal structures, often topped with a triangular cap. Sometimes there'd be five or six standing next to each other, not touching. *Adjacent*. Silos, Dad had explained, to store grain. The three of us stood at the bus stop like silos, not touching or communicating or revealing the inside of us, until Jack broke the silence.

"Oh, look at that. The three of us together the whole year. Won't that be fun?"

Curly hair plugged her headphones into each ear before turning her back to Jack. That left only me, and *fun* wasn't the first word to come to mind.

After much negotiating, Mom and Dad had agreed to say their goodbyes through the living room window instead of waiting with me at the bus stop. The blinds pulled right and then left as they fought to get the best view. The movement caught Jack's eye, and he turned as Mom waved, camera in hand.

"Parents," I mumbled, embarrassed.

I waited for Jack to get on the bus first, eager to put distance between us. I wasn't expecting him to be a front-seat sort of guy, and was lost in that thought when he stuck his foot in the aisle, launching me forward, my face hitting ground. I caught the scream before it escaped my mouth, my teeth clenched to hold it in. I turned around, but he was looking out the window. I touched my cheek where it throbbed. My fingers were wet from tears, not blood. I don't know which was worse. It wasn't the fall, it wasn't the pain—it was everything. I wanted to turn and yell at him, let out a few obscenities, tell him to leave me alone. But opening my mouth would release the rest of my tears. The last thing I needed on my first day was to let Jack see me cry. But with that nonresponse, on the very first day of school, I silently gave Jack permission to torment me.

"Keep it moving," the bus driver yelled. There's no way he could know my Cheerios were about to make a second appearance, and no one seemed to notice I was sweating a little too much for a slightly cool September morning.

I found a seat and put my backpack next to me, the universal sign for *don't sit here.*

At the next stop Jack's friends got on. I watched them, pretending not to watch them. Jack moved to the last row with them, kicking another boy out of the spot they decided would be theirs.

"Hey, Ahmed!" It was Jack. He was sitting two rows behind me. I didn't respond because I didn't know how to respond.

"HEY, AHMED," he said louder. When I was younger, I tried to teach people the soft *h* in Ahmed. Teachers, friends, the dentist, the general public. Like you're exhaling or sighing, I told them. But they always sounded like Darth Vader breathing into his mask, and I gave up. I wasn't about to correct Jack either.

"HEEEEEYYYYYY, AAAHMEEEEEEED!" I hated my name. "No time for a shower? Man, I can smell you all the way back here." And he broke into a cackle. *Maniacal.*

Why couldn't I come up with something to say? Something witty, quick, and funny. Something. Anything. It's hard to ignore someone when they're yelling inches from your ear, but that was my plan. Not a brilliant plan, I'll admit, but it was the only one I had. We made it to school. I was barely intact, and the school day hadn't technically started.

I remembered the scene in *Holes* when Stanley was sentenced to dig a five-foot hole every day, each day nothing but heat, thirst, and exhaustion. He stood in the scorching heat staring at his first finished hole. One of the boys comforted him by telling him the first hole was the hardest.

I understood what he meant. The first hole is the hardest.

CHAPTER
NINE

After that bus ride, the morning was a breeze. The sixth-grade classrooms were grouped together, giving me enough time to find my way between bells. There were so many first-day rules and expectation lectures, no one had time to notice me. Wasted worrying didn't stop me from future worrying. Lunch was next.

On the first day of school, every year, Mom packed us lunch, declaring a year of healthier eating. I saw her roll chapatis in the corner of my lunch box, leaving enough space for fish curry. She couldn't have chosen foods more likely to alienate me at the lunch table if she tried. *If you care what you eat, Ahmed, pack it yourself,* Mom would have said if I'd asked for something tame. A turkey sandwich with cheese. I don't even need mayo. Dad would have given me a non-smelly, boring, plain old sandwich. He grew up here; he got it. On the second day of school every year, Mom forgot all about it. It was tradition. On the first day of school every year, I dumped my home lunch and got in line at the cafeteria. That was tradition too.

I picked up my tray. So far so good.

"Turkey or meatloaf?"

"Meatloaf," I replied.

I pushed the tray along and picked a few things without looking up. It could have been liver and broccoli and I wouldn't have realized. Tray in hand, I looked around the cafeteria.

If every teen movie was to be believed, I was not ready to face the next half hour. Prickles of sweat dotted the back of my neck. The room was noisy and chaotic. Dinner rolls were tossed, music blared, kids danced. Seriously. There was even a stage at the front of the room. *Cacophony.* I don't remember lunch being like this at my school, but things were louder from the outside than the inside.

A spot opened at the end of a table. From the age of five, whenever I was nervous or anxious, Dad's advice was always "Fake it till you make it." "They can't tell what you're feeling unless you show them," he'd say. Usually I answered with an eye roll, but not today. Today, I faked it. I sat down like I wasn't nervous at all, like I belonged. I looked over what I had collected: meatloaf, a fruit bowl, green beans, and a roll. Not bad for blind picks.

I teetered on the edge of the bench, trying not to fall but leaving space between me and the others. My goal was to get through lunch and get to class. In class there would be a spot for me, and I wouldn't have to carve out my own space.

"You must be the new kid." The voice was rough and gravelly, the voice of someone about to stuff a kid's head into the toilet.

My plan to survive being the new kid was to blend in, not to get noticed. Stepping off the bus, I knew my plan would never work. It's hard to camouflage with white.

"Yup, you guessed it." I looked up and was surprised to see the face that belonged to the voice. He had arms like twigs, fuzzy blond hair, maybe the thickest glasses I'd ever seen, and a face like a six-year-old's.

"I'm Carl. I heard there was a kid moving here from Hawaii, but I thought you'd be more surfer dude, less math geek," he said.

"I've never surfed in my life. And actually, not that great at math either." I slid over enough to prevent an embarrassing fall.

"I get it. I've never been on ice skates and never watched

a hockey game. That's the Minnesota equivalent."

I pushed my meatloaf around before forcing a bite. The back of my neck cooled where the sweat dried.

"How do I find Mrs. Gaarder's room?" I asked. "It's not with the other classrooms."

A smile spread across Carl's face, lifting his glasses to his eyebrows. He pushed his glasses back down. "You're in accelerated Language Arts? Hey, me too! I'll take you there." A piece of green bean sprayed out of his mouth and landed near my hand. He took a second to swallow. "Did you read all the books? It was weird how they were so different when I read them in elementary school. I'm kind of excited about this class. Mrs. Gaarder is a legend around here. I've been hearing about that trophy for years. This year we're going to take her down."

A loud crash at the front made me look up. The dancers onstage lay in a pile on the floor until the girl on top stood up, freeing the others. They laughed.

"Well, I started *Holes*, but I haven't been able to find the book since I got off the plane. I haven't finished it," I replied.

His eyes widened. "Really? You know, if we left right now, we could make it to the library, get you a new copy, and still make it to class."

I had no intention of finishing the book, but I wasn't

going to admit that to the only person willing to talk to me. We emptied our trays, food uneaten, and left for the library. I had now been to the library more times in sixth grade than the entire fifth-grade year. Both of us crouched at the bottom shelf. Just once I'd love to find a book at eye level. He shuffled forward on his knees, finger-tapping each author on our way to the right one, and I followed behind, a faithful puppy waiting for his master to find him a treat. Only this treat was like a shot at the vet. *RW, RY, SA, SB*. Carl knew his way around the library, but luckily for me there were no copies of *Holes* available.

"Oh man," Carl said. "What are we going to do?" He seemed to be mixing me up with someone who cared.

"I hadn't gotten very far into the book anyway. There may be a copy of *Bridge to Terabithia* here, or the other book. I can't remember its name. Why don't we get one of those?"

My feigned interest in getting the work done seemed to make Carl feel better. There was one copy of *Terabithia* left. The front page was hanging on by a thread. Literally. When I tried to flip through it, a few pages fell to the floor. I picked them up and shuffled them together. The title page had a faded blue stamp on it.

"This book was donated to the Cedar Valley Middle

School by Mohammed Aziz."

Every hair on my body stood on end.

The librarian took the book, holding it by its corner. "You know, we'll have more copies in a couple of days when we're done unpacking things."

"No," I replied, "I'll take this one."

CHAPTER
TEN

We made it to class before the bell. Carl wanted a front-row seat, and I, of course, was more comfortable in the back. We settled on two seats in the middle.

Mrs. Gaarder was writing her name on the smartboard in pink. *Janet Gaarder*, she wrote in big curlicue letters. This was what a legend looked like, I guess. I wasn't impressed. She put her tablet down and turned around. There were no aunties trying to kiss me and no buffet curry smell, but I recognized her. Mrs. Gaarder was Janet. As in Pearson's Nut Goodies, Ziploc bag of fall leaves and maple syrup Janet. I mean Mrs. Gaarder.

Why didn't Dad tell me? I had left my home, my friends, and my school. I didn't need any more surprises. He should have known.

Mrs. Gaarder stood quietly at the front, and without saying a word, the class settled down. She looked at me, and the corners of her mouth lifted slightly with a flicker of a smile. Of recognition? To explain? In apology? She looked different under the white of classroom lights. She looked younger than Dad. Her hair was light brown and stringy, falling past her shoulders. Her eyes were too big for her face, and her nose too small for it. "I hope you're as excited as I am to get go-*ing*," she started. "I also hope you had a chance to read all the bo-*oks*." Her voice was warm and gooey, like her mouth was crammed full of brownie, and she almost sang the last word of each sentence, her voice going up a little higher at the end.

"I'll give you a few minutes to divide yourselves into groups of four. I don't want groups formed based on friendships. I don't want groups formed because you know one poor soul will do all the work. I want the groups to be fair. I'm sure you can figure out how to do that on your *own*."

It was hard to get over the fact that Mrs. Gaarder was Janet. I knew Janet. I knew her letters, her gifts, her stories.

Whenever Mom had a new friend visiting, I'd pray they wouldn't come with their children. If they did, there would be the dreaded "You two are almost the same age. Why don't you go play?" We were never close to the same age. And go play? Really? Instead we'd sit in my room silent and uncomfortable. I had the same feeling when I saw Mrs. Gaarder, except I was wishing she *was* a stranger.

We sat there, no one moving, no one saying a word. Someone coughed. Papers were shuffled in the back. She turned around deliberately, purposely looked at the clock, and turned through a full circle to face us again, like a ballet dancer. She lifted her index finger and wagged it side to side like a metronome. Ticktock, she was telling us. And like lumps of flesh with no brains, we stared at her. If I didn't focus, I could end up in the wrong group. I was counting on attaching myself to some hardworking sucker. The kid with notebook open, already taking notes, was a sure bet. That had been my MO since first grade, successfully avoiding many learning experiences. And I was turning out fine.

Finally Carl stood up.

"Okay, people," he said, his finger up and down counting us, "there are seventeen of us, so we will need three groups of four, and one group with five. Let's count off from one to four. All the ones, pull your desks to that side of the room. All the twos over here; the threes can stay over there, and the fours can take that end." He pointed to different sections of the room as he spoke.

I cringed for Carl. Everyone stayed in their chairs, not moving. Carl was dashing everyone's hope of doing exactly what Mrs. Gaarder had asked us not to. Carl, however, was unrelenting. I'm guessing choosing Carl as a partner would be a sure bet as well. He pointed at someone. "You're a one." And the count crept through the class, unwillingly dividing us into four groups. Four fair, too-bad-you-can't-be-with-your-friend groups. There's twisted justice when everyone walks away from a situation unhappy. The last person counted out her "one," and there was silence again. Both Carl and Mrs. Gaarder looked at us expectantly.

"Come on, people. Move it!" Carl yelled.

Desks scraped against the floor and backpacks were lifted as the class rearranged itself, and like that math puzzle game where you slide all the numbers around until you get them in order, everyone found their spot.

I was a three. It felt like a good, strong number. The sort of number where everyone else would do the work. I pulled my desk next to a girl who had already found her way to our spot. She had long blond hair that fell over most of her face. She wore a sports jersey with a name on the back that I was guessing wasn't hers. Jablownski. The name evoked the image of a man with a broken nose and missing front teeth. The light caught her braces, and every rubber band in her mouth was a different color, like talking into a rainbow. She had three angry, red, about-to-burst pimples in a triangle on her forehead. I understood right away why she let her hair fall in her face.

One morning I woke up with a painful bump on the tip of my nose, like a witch's wart. I wasn't surprised my first pimple decided to show up like that. On the tip of my nose, on picture day, so an eternal reminder could be framed and hung at home. Dad showed me his family album to try to reassure me. His seventh-grade photo with every strand of perfectly straight hair in place, his perfect skin glowing. Not reassuring at all. What he was trying to show me was on another page, his brother in fifth grade. He had a big, red, angry pimple in the middle of his forehead. Early acne, Dad pointed out, something else I had in common with my uncle. My dead uncle. That's probably what killed him. So if I had hair long enough, I would have hidden behind it too. It was one of the options I had considered.

"Hey, I'm Jessica," she said.

"Ahmed," I replied.

A boy who was probably not thinking about his dead uncle's acne at that moment rolled his wheelchair to join us. "Are you the suckers doing all the work this year?" he asked with a big grin on his face.

"You've known me too long to dare, Ari," Jessica replied.

"Geez, relax for a second, Jessica." He turned to me and put his hand out. I don't think I'd ever been offered a hand to shake. "I'm Ari, by the way. You must be the new guy."

"Yup, Ahmed." I didn't know what else to do, so I shook his hand.

Another desk pulled up behind me, but I didn't get a chance to turn around, make introductions, and possibly shake another hand. Maybe this was a hand-shaking sort of school.

Mrs. Gaarder took her place in the middle of the room, and with all four groups forming a rough U around her, I expected someone to hand her an orchestra baton. She picked up the trophy from the corner of her desk. It was a little golden cup—emphasis on little, no emphasis on golden. It was four inches tall, and the color of No. 2 pencils. She blew imaginary dust off the top. She opened her mouth in an O to blow warm air on it before polishing it on her shirt.

"Hey, that's no Stanley Cup," I said to Jessica, pleased with myself for having looked up what the Stanley Cup was. I thought it was named after Stanley from *Holes*. So wrong.

"You think?" Jessica replied. "They don't have sarcasm where you come from, Ahmed?" They had plenty where she came from.

Mrs. Gaarder cleared her throat.

"So, here's what we're going to doo-*ooo*," Mrs. Gaarder started. "We're going to take turns discussing all three of these wonderful books. When we've finished digging deep into your brains for the most trivial bits of intelligence and we've delved into crevices of thought that you didn't know existed, then and only then will we move on. Questions?"

She looked around for a raised hand.

"Okay, rules about the contest this year." She handed out papers, starting and finishing her journey in front of me. She paused at my desk, hand on the paper, waiting for me to look her in the face. I wasn't ready for eye contact yet, and she moved on.

She wasn't kidding about the rules. There were paragraphs and bullet points.

"All the details are there, but we'll go over the main points. I don't know what you've heard, but there are changes this year."

Carl had a highlighter and was already marking up the rules. I kid you not. He wasn't the only one, either.

"For the first time," Mrs. Gaarder started, "there will be points for group participation this year. At the end of each class I will tally who has contributed the most to our discussions, and they will get extra *points*." She had a copy of the rules on the smartboard and pointed to the correct section. "Participation will be based on two things." She held up one finger. "First, you will be graded on day-to-day participation, and I encourage everyone to contribute to the discussions. Each team must also appoint a leader, a moder-*ator*. It is the moderator's job to represent the ideas of their team. There will be one bonus point awarded per day for the moderator with the most articulate discussion points." She held up a second finger. "Second, each moderator has to lead a discussion on one of the three books. You'll be graded on how that discussion goes. On how well you involve others, how you lead."

She scrolled to the next section. "There are chances for individual points as *well*. When we are finished discussing each book, there will be a test." Everyone groaned. "Oh, you may want to save the groan, because it gets worse. There will be a test, but there will also be a short *ess*-ay." Mutiny. Voices raised. Chairs shifted. She waited for everyone to settle down. "For each book, you will be required to answer one of three questions that I will post online. If you don't have the Connect app already, I suggest you download it to-*day*."

She walked across the room.

"What you won't see this year is an opportunity for bonus points beyond this. The students last year almost set the school on fire with their proj-*ect*. Even though I'll miss the creativity, I'd like to keep us all safe." Everyone laughed except me.

"On the day of the contest, there will be one final chance to collect points. And as you know, whoever has the most points competes against me to try to win that trophy."

She turned off the smartboard.

"Let's start by choosing the moderators for each group. Any volun-*teers?*"

Of course not.

And then, from across the room, I saw Carl raise his hand. I would have reconsidered a friendship with him if I wasn't desperate.

"Wonderful," Mrs. Gaarder said. "We're off to a great sta-*art.*"

Our group sat looking into our laps. Sara and I did this all the time when Dad asked us to take out the trash or empty the dishwasher. We hoped that lack of eye contact could save us from that moment when you want to volunteer just to break the deafening silence. But I was no amateur. Years of letting Sara take the hit had strengthened me for this exact moment. I was settling into the quiet with the practiced patience of a yogi when from behind me I heard a voice that had quickly become familiar.

"Ahmed, the new kid. He said he wants to do it."

I turned so quickly, my chair tipped on two feet. It was Jack. He had his hood up and was slouched down. I hadn't seen him since the bus, wasn't expecting him in an accelerated class, and didn't think I was unlucky enough to have him in my group. I had let my guard down.

"I didn't hear Ahmed say anything. Do you want to volunteer, Ja-*ack*?" Mrs. Gaarder asked, pronouncing my name perfectly.

"No." You could barely hear his voice. "But Ahmed"— and his voice got louder—"had mentioned on the bus today that he wants to get really involved in Language Arts this year. Why don't you ask him? If he needs convincing, I can work on him on the way home today. We live near each other, so I can get to him any time." Did no one else notice the tone in his voice? *Menacing.*

"Is this true, Ah-*med*?"

I thought of the way I responded to Jack in my garage. I thought of the way I responded to him on the bus. This would have been the perfect chance to stand up to him.

"Umm, yeah. It sounds like fun," I answered. It definitely did not.

The other groups took turns finding volunteers. I use the word *volunteer* loosely.

"Per-*fect*," Mrs. Gaarder replied. "We are all set. Take the rest of class to figure out how you're going to organize yourselves and when you're going to meet. Those meetings should focus on agreeing on topics for discussion, but also as a sort of study group for the tests and essays. But your first task is to decide with which book we will start."

Everyone turned to Carl. There was a kid nicknamed X-Ray in *Holes*. It surprised me how he wasn't the biggest or the strongest, but still became the leader of the gang. Carl reminded me of him. He stood next to Mrs. Gaarder. "Okay, as moderators, we can decide which book to start with. Let's start with you, Ahmed."

He was giving me a fighting chance. Carl probably had notes color-coded and organized in laminated folders. I'd read half of *Holes* but didn't have a copy. I did have a copy of *Bridge to Terabithia*, and even though I hadn't started it, there was the potential of finishing it. Actual work done versus potential work. I'd known myself for twelve years. I had to bank on actual work done.

"*Holes*," I told him.

"Are you sure?" he asked, throwing me another lifeline,

knowing which book I had in my backpack.

"Yup."

He turned to the moderator of the next group. "*Holes* works fine for us." All the groups agreed, and the book was chosen.

Mrs. Gaarder pulled down a screen in front of one of the boards so it wound up tight, revealing what was hidden behind. "And now our journey begins." There was a simple maze drawn on the board, an easy path from point A to point B. There were three stops along the way, each marked with a cutout of a book. A laminated cutout of Mrs. Gaarder's face with the word *Champion* across it stood ready at the top, next to photos of grinning toddlers numbered one, two, three, and four. I guess those were supposed to represent us. At the end of the maze was a trophy. The cutout version was more impressive than the actual one.

Most of the class laughed. Someone booed. Everyone got ready to work.

"Ahmed, would you mind coming to my desk for a moment?" Mrs. Gaarder asked. As the noise rose, it was difficult to hear her.

"I know this is a surprise."

"Yeah, you could say that."

"Is it weird?"

"Yeah, you could say that."

Mrs. Gaarder squinted a little. "Your dad really wanted to warn you, but if you didn't figure it out, I didn't want you to know."

I shrugged.

"I didn't want you to think you could get away with not doing the work before the first day because you knew me."

Too late.

"I can tell you're upset. I should have known. I'm sorry, Ahmed. I should have let him warn you."

"I think I should get back to my group, Mrs. Gaarder."

Moderators with questions formed a line behind me. I didn't have any. Or I had too many.

"Okay, Ahmed."

A teacher had never apologized to me before. Maybe that's what made her a legend.

I turned my desk to face the others. Jack tried to say something, but Jessica interrupted him. "There it is," she said as she picked up a purple hair tie from the floor. "I was wondering where it went." She tied her hair back, her face exposed, her acne for everyone to see.

I looked away, but Jack stared at her. "Whoa, Jessica, you've got a little acne situation going on there."

Ari and I froze. Do I say something? Come to her aid? Stick up for her?

"What? Where? Huh?" She pretended to be confused

as she patted all over her face. "Do I have a little pimple somewhere? Oh no, how utterly embarrassing!" she said in an overly sarcastic way. "Thank you, Captain Obvious."

Jack didn't respond.

"Come on, let's figure out when we're going to meet," she said, and we spent the rest of the class working out the details.

Forget me coming to her aid—I had a feeling she would have to come to mine.

CHAPTER
ELEVEN

By the time I got home, Sara was going a hundred miles a minute. ". . . And it was so awesome, Dad, you should have seen it. Mrs. Anderson has all sorts of animals in her room like fish but also small birds and turtles and all sorts of things. And Anita . . . did I tell you she was my best friend . . . Anita said we each get our own tadpoles later. It's going to be incredible! Mom, there's a contest to see who gets to take the turtles home at the end of the school year. Can I bring one home? Please?"

Apparently Sara and I had very different first days.

Mom looked up from the pot she was stirring. Whatever she was cooking smelled like body odor with a hint of dead mouse. I preferred the days when Dad had enough energy to be the main chef, and not just cleanup crew. Dad made the most incredible rack of lamb and chicken curry. Mom made an incredible phone call to have pizza delivered. She believed creativity made up for skill in the kitchen. As an innocent bystander and unwilling witness, I can confirm that it does not.

"Assalamu Alaikum, Ahmed. How was your first day?" Mom asked.

"What's for dinner?" I replied, ignoring her question and her greeting.

"Pasta." Dad turned from the sink, hands covered in soap suds. He held the edge of the sink to steady himself, a little weaker than last month. "And tell us about your first day." No way the smell coming off that pot was pasta.

"It was fine."

"Fine?" Dad asked. "That's it? No interesting classes? No familiar teachers? Just fine?" He held his arms up, elbows bent like a TV surgeon, soap traveling down his arm.

"It would have been nice to know who Mrs. Gaarder was." There, I said it.

Mom turned off the stove and covered the pot with its lid, but that smell couldn't be contained.

They looked at each other, and then at me, and I could tell they were upset. "We wanted to. Really. But Janet was afraid you'd be worried all summer that you were going to be treated differently. She wanted you to know that you'd be comfortable in class with her as the teacher."

She's right that I might have worried about being the teacher's pet, but I still would have liked to know.

"Didn't you see all the photos on the walls? Did you see any of me? My brother?"

Dad waited, water dripping on the floor; Mom paused, hand still on the pot. This would have been a good time to tell them about Jack, about finding the book with my dead uncle's name in it, about how they fooled me about Mrs. Gaarder, but it didn't mean I was going to do the work. But Dad was excited, and Mom was hopeful, and I'm a wimp. So I changed the subject.

"The kids are weird."

"Oh yeah?" Dad asked.

"They shake hands, they're actually excited about Mrs. Gaarder's class, and even like Morning Report."

"What's Morning Report?" Mom asked.

I took a cookie from Sara's plate, and she slapped my hand away.

"Pretty much what it always is. Announcements, birthdays, a pathetic joke. They have all this great technology but don't know how to use it. A little bit of editing could have gone a long way."

Mom pointed the knife at me. "Maybe you can be the

one to make it better."

"Good one, Mom," I said sarcastically. Like I'd ever join a club.

"Sounds like you're going on a retreat next week. To Camp Burn," Mom said. "They sent us a permission slip to sign. Could be fun."

Dad turned back to the sink and laughed, shaking his head. "They're still taking kids to Camp Burn? Man, nothing has changed in all these years. Are you excited?"

Sure. Because going on a field trip when I didn't have anyone to hang out with sounded exciting. "I'm going to my room. Call me for dinner." I took another sniff of the pasta that hung in the air. "Or don't. Whatever."

That night I lay in bed, not able to fall asleep. Maybe it was the metallic aftertaste of the dinner that was resistant to brushing and even mouthwash. (Really, Mom? Chaat masala in the pasta?) Or maybe it was the idea of spending the next year leading an English group that had Jack in it. I read the inscription in my copy of *Bridge to Terabithia* again before tucking it under my pillow, the bump under my head somehow reassuring.

In a class of overachievers, maybe the only way to blend in would be to do the work. If that's what it took to survive, I'd have to make the sacrifice.

CHAPTER
TWELVE

I spent most of the week dreading the field trip. I never understood school field trips. If you were too lazy to teach us anything, let us sleep in. Of course, no one cared what I thought.

I grabbed my lunch bag off the counter, not wanting to consider what horrors lay within, almost knocking down Dad's pills. All Dad seemed to do these days was take pills and naps. He could have done both of those in Hawaii. And I wouldn't have to be nervous about a field trip.

The entire sixth grade shuffled and pushed to find their names on lists, dividing us by buses and assigning us to seats. It'd be nice if I was near someone I knew. Carl. Or Ari. Even Jessica. But field trips felt designed to weed out those of us without friends.

A girl in a bright pink T-shirt dropped her lunch on the seat next to mine and waved at someone a few seats back. "No fair!" she screamed in my ear. "You guys get to sit next to each other?" She looked at me and slumped down in her seat. "Great." Hey, I wasn't loving this either, you know. I pretended to look through my lunch.

But this girl, she wasn't a quitter like me. She spent the whole bus ride with her knees on the seat facing backward, trying to be part of her friends' conversation.

The buses unloaded us at camp and drove off to carry other kids to their days of torture. Five people wearing matching toothy smiles and green shirts, with clipboards and whistles, stood ready to lead us in our day of forced togetherness. *Camaraderie.*

"Okay, everyone, settle down. You have to listen for a few minutes, and then you're off to a day of fun and you'll be rid of us grown-ups . . . for the most part." I could tell she thought she was funny. Her lips turned up a little at the corners, like she was trying not to laugh at her own joke. People who thought they were funny when they weren't—they were the worst.

"There are three choices of activities for you today," the guy next to her started, like giving us a choice made us enjoy ourselves more. I choose being in bed. "You can climb up a huge rope ladder." Funny girl pretended to climb a ladder. "And cross a rope bridge." She pretended to walk across a tightrope. Umm, no thanks. "You can zip-line, flying like Superman." She put the arm with the clipboard in front of her and lifted one leg behind her. Umm, double no. "Or you can do the cup activity on the west lawn." She stood on her toes and pretended to dodge things on the ground, avoiding danger. At least that one sounded like I wouldn't have to be airborne. I signed up.

Apparently making sure there was ground under your feet wasn't a priority. There were only six names on the list. Carl saw me across the crowd and tried to scream across everyone's head, but I couldn't hear him. He lifted himself up on the shoulders of two guys in football jerseys. Carl had a way of making people do things even if they didn't want to. "The zip line is fantastic, Ahmed. Come try it."

Jack was there with a few of his friends. "Yeah, Ahmed. Come try it." I pictured Jack loosening my harness and me plummeting to my death.

"Umm, you guys go ahead." I liked Carl, but I wanted to live through this field trip.

It was easy to find the west lawn. All I had to do was look for the spot with the smallest number of people gathered. Ari was already there. "Hey, why'd you choose the most boring activity?" he asked.

"I don't know. Why did you?"

He pointed at his legs, limp in the wheelchair. ""Disability access doesn't always mean disability access." I felt stupid for asking.

Jessica playfully slapped the back of Ari's head. "Hey, if we got Jack over here, we could start a study session for Mrs. Gaarder's class."

"Jessica, you?" I asked.

"Wow, we've got a real Shakespeare here. Yes, Jessica, me," she said, imitating a monkey and pointing to herself. She put a hand on my head and said, "Yes, Ahmed, you."

One of the green-shirt clipboard guys walked down the hill to join us.

"What I was trying to say," I explained, "is that I would have expected you to be at one of the activities where you were flipping in the air or flying in the sky."

We walked to the table where green shirt waited. "Nah, I don't like to give up control like that."

Ari laughed. "A little secret I'm going to let you in on, Ahmed, is that Jessica tries to look braver than she is. Since preschool. She talks big and acts tough and has most people fooled. But those of us who have known her since she was little know the truth. She's a good faker."

Jessica pretended to tip Ari's wheelchair to the side. "Right about now I bet you're regretting letting me touch your wheelchair."

Scattered on the ground in front of us were a hundred clear plastic drinking cups filled with liquid of different levels and colors.

"All right, all right," the man in green who never thought to introduce himself said. "It looks like we've got a great group here today." If you say so. "We are going to have so much fun with this team-building activity." Quite the team. Ari in his wheelchair, Jessica standing with both her hands on her hips trying to look threatening, a guy with his finger up his nose, a few others, and me.

"Okay, okay. We need a volunteer," green shirt said. I was done volunteering. Ari raised his hand.

"Umm." The guy looked uncomfortable. "Maybe someone else . . ."

Ari smiled at me. "I love making them squirm."

"Let's go. Let's go. I need a brave individual," green shirt continued. "Someone willing to take a few risks." I was definitely out.

Jessica raised her hand.

"Wonderful. I hope you're willing to let your friends take control . . ." She put her hand down and stepped back. "Well, I'm out."

Green shirt stood in front of the guy with his finger up his nose, and the kid stared right back, not bothering to take his finger out. Not caring what others thought of you, not apologizing when you're caught with your finger up your nose—that's true bravery. I stepped forward to get a better look. Green shirt swooped down with a blindfold the same color as his shirt.

"Thank you, thank you," he said as he blindfolded me, pulling it tight. That was twice I had volunteered against my will. He put his arms on my shoulders while he explained the rules. "So you, the friends, the team, the group . . . have to help this guy." He squeezed my shoulders, so I knew he was talking about me.

He directed me a few steps forward, blindfolded. I tripped and he steadied me. Jessica laughed. Someone snorted. Not the kid with his finger up his nose, I'm guessing. I think you need both nostrils to snort.

"So"—he tried again to explain the rules—"the point is to get from this end to that end, blindfolded, without knocking over any cups."

It was weird to stand there and not see. When Sara was little, she played hide-and-seek by standing in the middle of a room and covering her eyes. She thought not being able to see us was the same as not being seen. This was a twisted version of the same thing.

"How am I supposed to get through if I can't see?" I asked.

"Aha. Aha. Great question." Really, it wasn't. "That's where your friends come in. They will guide you through it." Friends? "The record is one minute and twenty-eight seconds. That's the time to beat. And the time starts . . . now." He blew his whistle.

Jessica was the first to start, of course. "Okay, move forward about six inches." I stepped forward with my left foot and immediately felt a cup knock over.

"Oh geez," Jessica said, "what kind of person steps forward with their left leg?" This person, I guess.

My stomach churned, and a sour taste filled my mouth. The idea of everyone staring at me made me want to throw up.

"Let me try." It was Ari. "Lift your right foot, Ahmed, and take it about five inches to the right before putting it down."

My shoe slammed down firmly on a cup, sending them into another fit of laughter.

I was on display. I felt like I was caught in that dream where I'm in school wearing only my underwear, and everyone else was dressed.

"Wow, how big a deal is it, Ahmed, if your shoes are ruined?"

It felt like they had grown to the size of giants, towering

over me, pointing and laughing. "Not a big deal," I whispered.

My mouth was dry, and my legs shook a little.

"Sure?"

I wanted this misery over as quickly as possible.

"Sure."

They continued to guide me, and I hit cup after cup while they laughed. I wanted to scream at them to stop. I wanted to scream at green shirt. Wasn't it his job to make sure they weren't laughing at me?

"Hey, come check this out," Jessica yelled. And more voices were added to the laughter. I followed their words exactly, to the inch, but cup after cup fell. They were doing it on purpose. They were trying to make me look stupid, and I was obliging. I tried to peek under the blindfold, but green shirt thought that was the time to step in.

"No cheating." Not repeating himself this once.

More voices were added, more laughter. I recognized Carl's voice in the mix. I expected more from him. I thought he was different.

"To your left."

"Two steps ahead."

"Turn right. Your *other* right."

I was ready to pull the blindfold off and run away, when

the whistle finally blew. "Four minutes and twenty-two seconds," green shirt yelled. I pulled the blindfold off. Behind me, every single cup lay tipped over. I looked down at my shoes, and they were soaked through in red and yellow and pink and blue.

There were more people at the sidelines now, and they were high-fiving and laughing and patting each other on the back while they recounted the story of how they almost missed one in the corner but made me go back for it. Even green shirt laughed, whistle bouncing on his chest, clipboard at his side. And I stood there with the blindfold around my neck and my colored shoes. I imagined myself melting into a puddle and seeping into the grass. A brown puddle, which meant that I was finally the right color.

The laughter died down. "Okay, let's get lunch," Ari said. "I wish we had our phones. I would have loved to see the video of that. It could have gone viral." The crowd started to move. I could hold myself together for a few seconds more, waiting to be as alone as I felt so I could let my shaky legs give out and fall into a heap on the ground. But not until they left.

Jessica yelled at me, "Come on, Ahmed, let's get lunch." What?

Carl waved me over. "Let's eat. I bet we have the best

story out of everyone at lunch. I can't believe you didn't miss a single one."

They weren't ganging up on me?

Green shirt had a big smile on his face. "Well, well. That's a first. I guess there's more than one way to play a game."

I was in on the joke?

Ari was next to me. "I can't believe how cool you were. I couldn't have done that."

"Yeah, I guess stuff like that doesn't bother me."

I had faked it so well, I had faked myself.

CHAPTER
THIRTEEN

The way I saw it, to do the very least as moderator, I had to lead one discussion and raise my hand a few times. The very least is my favorite amount of work to do. Still, I would need a copy of the book.

The school was laid out like a big square doughnut, which made it easy to navigate, and I found my way to the library with only a few wrong turns. I opened the front cover of every copy of *Holes*, looking and not finding that stamp in the front before checking one out.

I passed the middle of the doughnut with its open space and a small brick path with trees and flowers; an open classroom, they called it. In a few months it would be buried in snow. I wondered if they still made you go out there. I wouldn't put it past them. In Hawaii, any classroom could be an open classroom. Just open a window.

That wasn't the only difference. The halls were narrower than I was used to, there was carpet on the floor, and as Dad had mentioned, there were photos everywhere. I mean everywhere. Hundreds or probably thousands of pictures of students from across the years covered every single wall. They probably had to take one down to hang a new one up. It must have been someone's brilliant idea to get us ungrateful kids to respect history, but I found it creepy. One hundred years of faces stared at me everywhere I went. Some of the pictures were grainy, with a handful of boys and girls wearing pants too short and skirts too long. Some were more recent, with kids in snow pants making goofy faces and bunny ears. Why were black-and-white photos always serious, as if draining the color drained the smiles?

No one paid attention to those photos. There was barely enough time between bells to open my locker, get my books, and move on without contemplating the history of the school, but I scanned them when I got a chance. In all those white faces, smiling or not, I was looking for something familiar. Eventually I found it.

It was above my locker, with a white border and thin black frame like the rest of them, right over my head. There was no caption on this one, but in a row of blond-haired, blue-eyed, tall kids, he was the only short one.

Like me. He was the only one with black curly hair. Like mine. He was the only brown kid. Like me. He had a crinkle between his eyebrows from frowning. Like I do. In a sea of kids who knew to say cheese, he did not. He was the only color in that picture, but he had the serious expression of a black-and-white photo. *Ironic.* There were photos of Dad's brother on his dresser. The two of them in the bath, shampoo lathered like cones on their heads. Both of them in a mosque flanking their father, hands crossed on their chests in prayer. My uncle. The same uncle whose copy of *Bridge to Terabithia* was under my pillow.

From the moment I noticed him, he became my guy. Each time Jack pushed me into my locker, I'd look at him. When I found my assignment, crumpled, at the bottom of my backpack just in time, he was the one who saw my relief. When the kid at the next locker talked about last night's hockey game, I looked at him. He got me. I was glad someone did.

CHAPTER
FOURTEEN

Ari, Jessica, Jack, and I were meeting in the cafeteria before school to work on our project. I had spent more time coming up with ways to get out of being the moderator than I had spent preparing for it. Classic me. In fact, despite the best of intentions, I hadn't finished the book. Old habits die hard.

Mom was driving me to school, and it occurred to me that I was skipping the pressure of being on the bus with Jack, only to get to school early to . . . be with Jack. Ridiculous.

Sara was curled up next to Dad on the couch, her head on his lap. He smiled and waved. Today was a big day. We'd find out if all those pills he had been taking had worked. I ran up to my room and put *Terabithia* in my backpack. Like a good luck charm. I patted my bag to feel better.

"Well, this is nice," Mom said, "I like that you're taking class seriously and making an effort. I've heard Janet is a great teacher."

Maybe Mom wouldn't be quite as impressed if she realized my motivation was self-preservation.

"Oh, I promised our neighbor I'd take her son to school as well. You must have met him on the bus. She said he's in your class."

My hand froze, seat belt in hand, midway across my chest.

"I can't remember, but I think his name is John or Zack. One of those one-syllable names."

"Jack."

"That's it, Jack. Do you know him?"

Do I know him? "Mom, there's no way we're taking Jack to school." Of course I knew him. "He's the worst. Like, the absolute worst." Only a few weeks into school, and I knew him a little too well. "We absolutely can't take him."

Mom stopped the car to look at me. "What do you mean?"

How could I explain Jack to my mom? How I felt uncomfortable around him, that I went out of my way to avoid him, that he was everything I hated about being in Minnesota.

"Well, he tripped me on the bus on the first day of school, Mom."

"Okay."

"And he made me volunteer to be moderator in Mrs. Gaarder's class."

"Okay."

"And he's just not nice."

"Okay."

When I said it like that, all in a row, I knew it didn't sound bad. But if I used the word *bully*, Mom would get involved. I didn't need that.

She turned the volume down on the radio.

"You don't have to be best friends with him. His mom came over and asked if I could help out. And I said yes. So we're taking him."

"But, Mom . . ."

"Listen, I'm not questioning what you said about him. But I also know his mom's a single parent, and she travels all the time. He's on his own a lot. That can't be easy. Not for Jack, and not for his mom. So if we can help by taking him to school early, we help."

I started to open the door. "Then let me out. You take precious Jack, and I'll take the bus or ask Dad to drop me."

Mom gave me that look that I didn't dare mess with. "Ahmed Aziz. You close that door this minute. You know your father isn't feeling strong enough to drive you, which is why I stayed late. If all of us are moving things around to take you to school early, you are going. And you are going to deal with being in the car for ten minutes with a kid you don't like."

I turned the volume back up so I didn't have to listen to her. But I also closed my door.

Jack was already waiting in his driveway for us, so I didn't have to go ring the doorbell for him. How considerate.

"Good morning, Jack."

"Good morning, Mrs. Aziz." He climbed into the back.

"I hear your mom is in Zimbabwe this week. How exciting. Seems like she goes to some unusual places."

He buckled his seat belt. How responsible.

"She was in Zimbabwe a few days ago, but I saw on her Instagram this morning that she is in Sudan. She moves around a lot."

Mom reversed out of his driveway, looking at Jack in the rearview mirror and me out of the corner of her eye.

"She said she's a photojournalist. So much more exciting than being an accountant like me." She laughed. "But you must miss her."

"I'm used to it. Someone comes to spend the night, but usually I get to watch as much TV as I want. Even with dinner. It's not bad." But the way Jack said it, something about the tone in his voice, made it sound bad.

I shifted in my seat and fiddled with my vent. I had managed not to say a word.

"Ahmed's dream come true," Mom said.

Mom was super strict about not turning on the TV at mealtime and all of us sitting down together for dinner. No matter how much we begged. Sara bugged me. Dad had endless questions about my day. Mom forced us to have family dinner time together. But I can't imagine them not being there.

She dropped us off at the back entrance where a few other suckers were getting head starts on their day. "Remember we'll be at the doctor's and won't be home when you get back. Don't worry, though, I'll be back in time to make dinner."

Yay, Mom's dinner. The abuses of this day seemed endless.

CHAPTER
FIFTEEN

Jack and I walking in together. Never in my dreams. Maybe in a nightmare.

"My mom's dinners are the worst. I'd much rather watch TV and eat a sandwich."

"Shut up, Ahmed. You don't know a thing about me."

Ari and Jessica were seated, notebooks out and ready to go, when we walked in. I looked at the clock; we were only three minutes late. I squeezed my chair between Jessica and Ari to avoid Jack, my knee pressed against the metal of Ari's wheelchair.

Jack tapped something into his phone. "Since Ahmed is moderator, he can take notes." He flickered his eyes from his screen to me, the pause giving me time to argue. I didn't oblige.

"How do you guys want to do this?" Ari asked. "It'd

be great if we got enough ideas for the group discussion as well as our own essays. I wish she'd tell us which team presents first."

I looked at our feet in that tight circle, almost touching, my tie-dye shoes in contrast to the whites and blues of the others.

"She knows we'd only work on the one we're in charge of presenting," Jessica said. "This way we're forced to prepare for all three."

"We could start by sharing our notes," Jack said. JACK SAID?!?! Jack had read the work? Made notes? Was contributing to the discussion?

I wasn't expecting that.

Jack pointed the sharp end of his pencil at me, stabbing the air. "Ahmed should start."

Now that I expected.

The cafeteria felt different this time of day. No students, no noise, no lunch line. Only the smell was the same; the smell of the cafeteria was as familiar as the smell of a gym locker. On the plus side, if I closed my eyes, I could pretend I was back in Hawaii.

"Sure. Umm . . . I kind of liked the part about Stanley being away from his home and family. I liked seeing him adjust as the new kid. That really interested me." That sounded like a least-amount-of-work sort of analysis.

"Really, did it?" Jessica said sarcastically, rolling her eyes. "Come on, Ahmed, we aren't in third grade. We've got to come up with something better than that." She turned the pages of her notebook until she found what she was looking for. "Stanley's family feels stuck because of a curse. That's fate. They feel nothing they do will work until the curse is broken. They have no free will." She ran her finger under a line of her notes. "Fate versus free will, that could be our discussion."

Other groups from Mrs. Gaarder's class trickled in. Getting kids to wake up early must be part of what made her a legend.

"I like that idea," Ari said. "We could talk about which characters believed in the curse and which didn't, and how it made a difference in their lives." He rolled his wheelchair back enough to release my knee. A chip left behind from yesterday's lunch crunched.

"Personally," Jessica said, "I really liked it when Stanley used sarcasm as a defense mechanism. Like when Mr. Pendanski asked Stanley whose fault it was that he was sent to camp, and he answered that it was the fault of his 'no-good-dirty-rotten-pig-stealing-great-great-grandfather.' That was funny." It reminded me of how Jessica responded to Jack's comment about her acne.

Jack tapped something into his phone, not looking up.

"Whatever," he said. "Everyone likes to have someone to blame for things they've done. I think Stanley's family actually liked the curse. It allowed them to blame someone else for their miserable existence."

"Ahmed," Ari said, resting his finger on my notebook, "you'd better start writing all this down so you know what to talk about in class."

Being near Jack made me nervous. Things that came naturally to me suddenly felt difficult. Things like ducking out of schoolwork, keeping a low profile, speaking in full sentences. I was the king of passing the buck and wasn't ready to be dethroned. "Jessica, wouldn't you rather be moderator?"

"No thanks," she said. "I get way too worked up. You don't want me up there." She turned her attention back to Jack. "If you don't like what I had to say, Jack, what's your brilliant idea?"

His phone buzzed, and he lifted it from his lap to look.

"I think your adoring fans can wait until we finish, Jack," Jessica said.

I raised my eyebrows but didn't dare ask. Adoring fans?

"Jack is famous for having the most friends and followers on Connect," Ari said.

"Connect? Like the homework app Mrs. Gaarder made us download?"

"Yeah, but it's also a school social media site. It's the school's weak way of trying to keep us safe online," Jessica explained.

Ari laughed. "It's got to be a full-time job keeping up with all those fans."

Jack ignored him. "We could talk about things being fair versus unfair. Almost everything that happened to Stanley and Zero was unfair. Maybe we could talk about that."

"Well, boo-hoo, Jack," Jessica replied. "Cry me a river. Isn't calling something unfair another way of putting blame on something besides yourself? Saying it's unfair is the same as saying it's a curse. Either way you're not taking responsibility for your actions. You're letting other things control you."

I scribbled notes in my book, trying to look busy.

"Ari, what about you? Have anything you want to add?"

"Yeah, so my ideas weren't quite as complicated as what you guys bring up. I wanted to talk about friendship in the book. I liked how Stanley and Zero became friends, and it made Stanley stronger and even saved their lives in the end."

Jessica leaned back in her chair and let out a long "Oh geeeeeeez." She put her head in her hands and let her hair fall to the front in case we hadn't completely grasped her utter exasperation.

"Hey, I kind of like that, Ari. How did it save their lives?" I wasn't going to let Jessica bulldoze everyone's ideas, because that's the kind of thing a good moderator would do. I think.

"Wait." Jessica sat straight up. "You haven't read the book?"

All three of them stared at me.

"Man, our grades really depend on this. Plus, I really, really want to win that contest and get that trophy. Like really." The others nodded in agreement. "We all do."

"Why is that tiny trophy such a big deal?" I asked, not pausing for an answer. "Maybe you need to get over it."

"No one is getting over it," Jessica said. "You'd better get with it instead. I'm not kidding."

CHAPTER
SIXTEEN

I was the first out of the cafeteria, getting out before Jack had a chance to concentrate on me instead of his phone. The halls were mostly empty when I got to my locker, just me and the guy who managed to magically get there before anyone else. I glanced at him and tried not to stare. He had intricate headgear. In fact, it was an architectural marvel of metal and plastic surrounding his neck and the top of his head. I couldn't tell what it was holding up or protecting. That had to be some pretty messed-up teeth if that was its purpose. Looking at that metal cage, I understood why he was always in and out of his locker first. I wouldn't want to hang out in the halls with that contraption either. I turned around to say hi, but he was already gone. I didn't think that much metal could also be stealth. I looked above my locker to share my surprise with my uncle, my *doppelgänger*.

Suddenly, I was pushed. Hard. I staggered forward, my arms windmilling to keep my balance before I found myself flat on the floor, my backpack at my feet. I was always in the wrong place at the wrong time. Call it fate like Jessica, or luck like Jack, but it was one more thing Stanley and I had in common.

"I feel sorry for you, Ahmed." Jack kicked my backpack a few feet in the air before it landed in the middle of the hall. His sidekicks smirking behind him. "I'm so glad my mom doesn't hover over me like yours." He stood over me, pushing both fists deep into his pockets. Like he wanted to threaten me but wanted to be casual about it, like it wasn't a big deal, like I wasn't worth the trouble of taking his hands out of his pockets. "Like a baby."

I was still on the floor, and Jack and his friends were standing over me, when Mrs. Gaarder walked past, deep in conversation with our math teacher. Jack reached for my hand and pulled me up. "Let me help you up, buddy," he said with a smile. Math teacher smiled back. Mrs. Gaarder didn't.

"Everything okay here?" she asked.

Jack put his arm around my shoulders. "Absolutely," he answered. "Just showing Ahmed our Cedar Valley spirit."

Math teacher continued to smile, so proud of his wonderful students. Mrs. Gaarder didn't. "Cedar Valley spirit includes getting to class on time," Mrs. Gaarder said. "You two should get going."

"Janet," I heard the teacher say, pulling her away, "you need to relax a little. That was a sweet gesture."

Mrs. Gaarder looked over her shoulder at me, her brow knit with worry.

I pressed my back against the locker, to make room as the halls filled, but also to hold myself up. Headgear guy weaved through the stream of people. It reminded me of those zebras in Africa, zigzagging to confuse their predator. My backpack was in one hand, its mouth wide open, and the torn copy of *Bridge to Terabithia* was in the other.

"This fell out and looks like it got pretty beaten up," he said. He handed me my backpack and book, but then kept standing there like he wanted to say more.

"You know, Jack is a jerk. It's that simple. Some guys are like that. My plan is to stay out of his way until my brace comes off in a couple of years. You need your own plan."

"In a couple of years," I answered, "I'm still going to be me."

I think he tried to shrug, but it was hard to tell through all that metal.

I held the book tight, as if it had the power to hold me together. The crowds thinned, and when the bell rang, everything went completely still. I didn't know what to do. Avoiding Jack didn't work. Not avoiding Jack didn't work. I was stuck. I kicked my locker lightly, and its clang echoed in the empty hall, making my reaction feel bigger than it was. Making me feel like I had actually reacted. I kicked a little harder, the locker door vibrating under my foot. Every kick making the sound my voice hadn't. I. HATE. BEING. HERE. Each word a metallic scream. My foot throbbed, and I pressed my head against the locker, feeling the cool of the metal against my forehead.

I felt a hand on my shoulder, but I wasn't ready to turn around and face them and whatever trouble I was sure I was in.

"Ahmed," Mrs. Gaarder whispered.

"Ahmed," she said again, her voice as warm as her hand. Warmth was home. I turned to her.

I don't remember walking to her office. She let me sit quietly and knew not to ask questions. She didn't tell me it was all going to be okay. She sat by my side and kept the warmth of her hand on my back.

"Do you want to talk about it, Ahmed?"

I shook my head no.

"Do you want me to call your mother?"

I shook my head no.

"Do you want to go to your next class?"

I shook my head no.

No to my dad being sick. No to being picked on. No to ever having moved here.

CHAPTER
SEVENTEEN

Sara didn't give me a chance to get inside the door before she started her story. "You're not going to believe what happened today. One of the mice got out of its cage and we ran all around school looking for it. I was the one who found it, in the girls' bathroom when I wasn't even looking. It ran out from behind the toilet after I flushed. I grabbed it and brought it back to class and all the kids stood up and cheered. I was a hero."

We continued to have very different school experiences.

I wasn't sure I had it in me to sit down and read *Holes*, but Jessica said she wasn't kidding, and I didn't want to find out what that meant.

I looked up when my phone buzzed with a text, and I was surprised to see that it was dark outside. Days were getting shorter.

Appointment running long. Won't make it for dinner. Order pizza. Cash in the drawer.

I had enough time, after calling for a large cheese pizza (hold the pineapple), to finish the book. I arranged pickled red peppers on it before calling Sara down.

At every birthday and school party as far back as I can remember, there was pepperoni pizza. In kindergarten it was hard to make the connection between pork I knew I wasn't supposed to eat and those perfect red circles. I wanted nothing more than to have pepperoni pizza like everyone else. Mom concocted her own substitution, cutting circles of pickled red peppers for our pizza at home, singing her own version of Peter Piper's peck of pickled peppers, adding pepperoni pizza to his story. The tongue twister was as fake as the pepperoni. *Counterfeit*. It was years before we knew the difference, and by then the habit stuck.

We sat, stuffed and nauseated from one slice of pizza too many, when I heard the car in the garage. The engine turned off, but only one car door slammed shut. Mom came in alone.

"How was the appointment?" I asked, looking behind her. "And where's Dad?"

"Give me a second," Mom said. "Let me get a cup of tea and we can sit down. It's good news."

Sara was skipping around the kitchen island, retelling

her story of the mouse, but the story had gotten bigger. She had to lunge and roll under the stall door to save the mouse, and her entry to the classroom was short of a ticker-tape parade. Mom smiled as she crushed her cardamom and cloves for tea. Despite all her culinary missteps, Mom's chai was worth the wait. Creamy, sweet warmth. A perfect antidote to feeling full and nauseated. She didn't have to ask before pouring it into three cups, and we gathered around. Tea, even in the middle of the night, was served in fancy cups and saucers in our house.

"We took Dad for his appointment today and met with a team of five doctors. They spent more than an hour going over all his tests and results. The pills they gave Dad worked!" Her eyes glistened with tears as she lifted her cup to her lips. "His virus is cleared and he's ready for surgery."

"He is?" I asked. "I can't believe it." It felt like we had been waiting for this forever.

"Or course he is," Sara said. She had never doubted it. She poured tea into her saucer and lifted it to her lips; like waves, the tea threatened to spill over one side and then the other. Dad had learned this trick, to make piping-hot tea cool down and immediately drinkable, from his grandfather. He did it everywhere, at other people's houses, in fancy restaurants, apparently even in his college cafeteria, where Mom saw him pour his coffee into a dessert plate. It was the way her family drank tea in India, and she jokes that's how she knew she wanted to marry him. Sara hadn't mastered the technique, and Mom absentmindedly opened her napkin and positioned it to catch what dripped.

"He'll be home tomorrow after they've done some more testing. They're very hopeful," Mom said as she stirred her tea, the spoon clinking against the cup. "Only two people have gone through this treatment before, and one of them is doing great." I stared into my cup where little bubbles of foam moved to the edge of the cup.

"What happened to the other guy?" I asked.

"What other guy, Ahmed?"

"Well, you said one person did well. What happened to the other person?"

She put her cup down. "I don't know," she replied. "They didn't say."

Mom has always been a terrible liar.

CHAPTER
EIGHTEEN

A surprise pep rally was the only thing worse than a regular pep rally. Plus, big surprise, I wasn't feeling very peppy. There should be a law against forced enthusiasm. We filed into the gym and filled the bleachers. The unexpected mid-October cold wasn't enough to cancel the rally, only to move it inside. People never know when to give up.

I was squeezed between two guys who seemed as excited about the rally as the cheerleaders onstage. They were up on their feet, in unison, with every cheer, and when they sat down the bleacher bounced, lifting me off my seat. Dad's preparation for surgery included green smoothies that smelled like gasoline, and long walks, forcing us to get in shape with him. The smoothie tasted like it smelled, and my stomach churned.

I scanned the crowd for a friendly face, a familiar face, while I bounced up and down at the whim of their cheers. Carl was on the gym floor, in charge of the microphones and the sound system. For a change he didn't look like he knew what he was doing. I could have helped him if I was sitting closer. I could have turned the volume down as well. Across the gym, Ari sat in front of the bleachers by himself. Disability access isn't always disability access. I understood what he meant.

Cheerleaders threw their pom-poms in the air, the band played and stomped their feet, someone in a beaver costume ran up and down the gym flapping his (her? its?) arms to get us to cheer. If an alien spaceship landed, they'd take off immediately, not interested in a population with subpar intelligence.

They introduced the team. Basketball, maybe? Football, perhaps? Hockey, could be? One by one, each member walked in with a parent next to them. The parents' proud smiles obvious even from the last row.

The first player, they announced, had a 4.0 grade-point average and was on three different teams. I recognized him from the "Student of the Month" segment of Morning Report. On the first day of school, they showed videos of him building houses in South America over the summer. Beaming mom and son walked in, holding hands, I kid you not. I think Mom would die of a heart attack if I asked to hold her hand. See, I was doing her a favor. The crowd cheered, and they lifted their combined hands in victory. But the game wasn't until that weekend, so I don't know what victory they were celebrating.

The microphones squeaked; Carl needed to adjust the sound mixer.

So-and-so volunteered at the animal shelter. Cheers.

So-and-so raised money for the homeless. Cheers.

Jack Hanson, they announced. The crowd cheered, and Jack walked in. Jack, they said, had a 4.0 grade-point average and had the biggest following on Connect. He walked in with his . . . science teacher. The teacher tried to hold Jack's hand in that sign of victory, but Jack flicked it away. They didn't run in unison to their folding chairs like the others. They walked quickly, and he sat down. The seat next to Jack was the only empty one on the gym floor.

Even if dad was in the hospital, he would have managed to be there to hold my hand and run through the gym. To make sure I wasn't the only one with an empty seat next to me.

The band stomped around again, the cheerleaders threw their pom-poms again, and the beaver flailed its arms again.

A screeching sound made the entire audience turn to look, only to see Jessica pulling up a chair next to Ari. Right in the middle of assembly. Ari looked embarrassed. Jessica didn't notice.

The two of them pretended to throw up when the band went by, not bothering to spell out the school name when the cheerleaders instructed them, and they didn't move when the flailing beaver got everyone else up. *Kindred.* They saw me across the gym, and I pretended a knife was stabbing me. I met my best friend, Adam, in second grade, when we were the only two who hated recess. Hating something in common can make friends as easily as liking something in common. I hoped. Ari and Jessica fake-stabbed themselves back.

CHAPTER
NINETEEN

I was somewhat prepared for class. If anything deserved a pep rally, that was it.

I held my breath, hoping the first turn wouldn't be mine.

"I have to step out for a minute. Get yourselves into your groups, and if I'm not back soon, start the discussion," Mrs. Gaarder said. It felt like she was speaking directly to me.

She had moved her laminated face farther down the maze on the board. All four toddler faces were stuck behind the starting line. The obsession with this silly contest and sillier trophy was beyond ridiculous. Silly didn't stop me from being nervous.

I reached for my headphones. I knew the drill—teacher out of the classroom meant free time. Apparently not with this overachieving bunch. Ari had his backpack on his lap.

"What're you doing?" I asked.

"Come on, move your butt. I felt like she was talking right to me." The other groups already had their chairs pulled together. "No one wants to disappoint Mrs. Gaarder. Get moving."

"Man, Ari, Mrs. Gaarder is like the warden in *Holes*."

"What are you talking about?"

"Well, everyone is scared of her, and she doesn't have to say or do a thing." I guess their reputations did the talking. I didn't expect Mrs. Gaarder to scratch someone's face wearing poisoned nail polish, but there were similarities.

"Hey, you read the book. Good job."

Our group felt smaller than the others, and I counted each group twice to convince myself we weren't. I tapped my toes quickly, right and then left, keeping count. If I tapped until twenty, maybe I'd feel less jittery. Okay, maybe thirty. I wish she had told us who was going to lead the discussion before she left the room. The other groups looked taller, they looked smarter; at the very least, they looked less sweaty. This was not going to go down well for me. Sixty toe taps.

"Hey, you've got all your notes, right?" Jessica asked.

"You remember everything we went over, right? You read the rest of the book, right?"

"Yeah, yeah, yeah, Jessica, but you know, it's not too late for you to take over and run this thing."

"No way."

"You've got this," Ari added.

In my entire existence, I don't think I had "got" anything less than I had "got" this. Maybe our group wouldn't get called first. I could do the math. There was a 25 percent chance that I would get called, which meant there was a 75 percent chance that I wouldn't. Maybe Carl would volunteer to go first. Maybe Mrs. Gaarder wouldn't make it back. Maybe there would be a fire drill.

The door opened, and she was already talking as she walked in. "So, what do you want to start with, Ah-*med*?"

Maybe, maybe, maybe. Maybe I should learn that luck would never be on my side.

The class shifted in their chairs to look at me, like they were one person. I understood what the dead in dead silent meant. I swung my legs to the side. They were jelly. As I pushed myself up from my chair, I looked at my arms, amazed they were able to lift me. I felt like I was floating above, looking down at myself. And I didn't look great. My hair, never my tamest feature, looked electrified, à la Einstein, if Einstein was a skinny brown boy with curly hair. I looked tiny and sweaty and shaky, and somehow like a giant too big for my chair. A tiny giant, like the Hulk just before he ripped through his clothes. Somehow those trembling, twiglike legs held me up, and like a miracle I began to speak. But I was definitely no Einstein.

I knew there were things we had decided to talk about. Something about fate and luck. I looked at my notes, but they were jumbled and foreign. I put them down.

"Today, um, I thought we would focus on Stanley, uh, the main character." I heard Jessica release her sigh. "*Holes* is all about Stanley. His whole family, going back to his great-great-grandfather, had a curse placed on them. Because of the, um, curse, Stanley is accused of a crime he didn't commit. He's then sent to Camp Green Lake, where he is forced to dig a five-foot hole every day as punishment." I paused. Not for effect, but to give myself a moment to think.

I could hear the clock tick, like school clocks do. It's no coincidence the word *tick* describes clocks and bombs. Both felt like a countdown to an explosion.

"At Camp Green Lake, he had to adjust to a life very different from the one he'd known," I continued, dismissing thoughts of time-bomb clocks. "He had to leave his home, where, like any of us, he was comfortable and loved." I faked a cough into my elbow to buy time. "He was sent to a camp that was essentially a jail. He was the new kid, and, um, Stanley reminds us how tough that is. There are so many reminders in the book about how difficult it can be as the new kid." Now I was officially rambling.

"Stanley spent the whole summer doing manual labor. And if digging a hole in the heat without much food and water wasn't hard enough, he had to do it with kids who were a lot tougher and meaner than him." If I didn't pause or take a breath, I could drown out the clock. I spoke faster. "Even if every situation isn't as difficult as Stanley's, being new can be tough. As the new kid here, that stood out for me in this book."

My voice started to get quiet, but I didn't let it. It occurred to me, in that moment, that could be why Mrs. Gaarder spoke the way she did. Maybe she had to push out her last words before she lost them. Maybe adults had to fake it too. My thoughts about Mrs. Gaarder were interrupted by Mrs. Gaarder. "That's a great place to start, Ahmed. Tell us what you mean and then we can open it up to the *class*."

"Well, Stanley is surrounded by kids who are criminals"—I picked up speed and volume, encouraged by the possibility of opening up the discussion to the class—"and he doesn't fit in. He's there because of a combination of a mistake, bad luck, and possibly a curse. He's not supposed to be there. He doesn't deserve to be there." I could have been talking about myself. "Even with everything he's going through, his worries are the same as ours. He wants to fit in. He wants the other kids to accept him and like him. He wasn't as worried about surviving camp as he was about making it through the day."

Without expecting to, I had let everyone see how nervous I was about being the new kid. Great.

"But, hey, it's like Stanley says," I added, trying to make things lighter than they felt, "the first hole is the hardest. So I guess it does get easier."

A girl with a mole in the center of her forehead like a bindi raised her hand. Sara fought with Mom once because she wanted to wear a bindi. Mom argued it wasn't right to use other people's religious traditions because you liked the way they looked. Sara spent days mad, complaining we weren't American enough, and now we weren't Indian enough, ignoring Mom's explanation of culture versus religion. The girl with her hand raised coughed impatiently, interrupting my bindi thoughts. Was I supposed to call on her? I suppose anything was better than babbling on, so I did.

"Someone else in the book," she said, "I don't remember who—said the second hole is the hardest, and then someone else said that the third hole is the hardest, and the fourth, and the fifth. Does that mean it never gets easier?"

"That's a good point. Does anyone have a thought about *that*?" Mrs. Gaarder stepped in and pointed to a boy in the front row, but I didn't give him a chance to answer.

"I think the author is trying to say that it's all about perspective. You can sit back and be a victim. Every day and every hole can be harder than the one before. Or you can realize that every hole you dig makes you a little stronger and wiser, so you are more prepared to deal with the next hole."

It was quiet in the room, and I took that moment to sit down. Jessica spent the rest of the class trying to bring up some of the themes from my notes and giving me dirty looks. I should have felt bad, but I was happy to be done. I had made it.

When class ended, I pretended to look for something in my backpack, to stall my exit and avoid facing everyone who now knew my feelings about being new.

"Hey, new kid . . ."

"Yeah," I answered. It was someone from Carl's group. Lucky guy.

I saw Mrs. Gaarder's head turn and freeze in the way adults do when they're pretending they're not listening but they are.

"I think we have our next class together. You want to walk with us?" Mrs. Gaarder's shoulders relaxed, as did mine.

"Sure."

After Stanley finally finished digging his first hole, tired and well after everyone else, he stood to admire it. When I read it, I had thought it was ridiculous, but now I got it. I was proud of my first hole too.

CHAPTER
TWENTY

Sara's bedtime was a firm eight p.m. and mine was a not-so-firm nine, which meant I had an hour to watch TV shows and play video games Mom thought were too inappropriate for Sara. Playing video games was fun, but watching Sara go to bed begging to play "just one game" was even better. Some nights I'd eat ice cream sundaes with Mom and Dad, and Sara's head would explode the next morning when she saw three bowls with dried chocolate syrup in the sink. They seemed more relaxed those evenings, more willing to say yes to requests that would have otherwise been met with a no. I used those evenings to negotiate the upgrade to my phone and convince them to let me quit piano lessons. It was the only time of day I learned anything useful.

"What's a guillotine, Mom?"

"A machine invented to efficiently chop off people's heads."

No "Where'd you hear that?" or "Why'd you ask?" or "Where's this coming from?"

So, obvious follow-up question: "Umm, why?"

She would start with the history of France, go into the reasons why the people revolted, and finish with an analysis of how crowds of people often did cruel things an individual person wouldn't. Made a guy sorry for asking.

Dad's answers were the opposite. *Meandering.* When I asked Dad why he went camping only once a year, and always on the thirteenth of March, he told me a long story about being alone with his thoughts, and contemplation, and "Sometimes in life . . ."

"But why March thirteenth, Dad?"

"Rivers run deep, and you have to give things space to bubble up."

But rivers aren't always deep, and they don't bubble up.

Mom is the one who told me, on one of those evening, ice-cream-fueled conversations, that March 13 is the day Dad's brother died, and Dad went camping every year to be alone, to remember his brother.

One March 13, Dad went camping and didn't come back. I remember the red and blue lights from the police cars flashing through our bedroom blinds, and Sara's midnight confusion when she was woken up by the sound Mom made when they came to tell us they had found him—part scream, part cry.

It was days before we were allowed to see him and weeks before a doctor would be sitting at the hospital whiteboard explaining how Dad was found unconscious because his liver had become too weak to clear toxins from his blood.

It was Mom who told me, on one of those evenings, that Dad had the same infection and the same liver disease that killed his brother.

"But couldn't it kill Dad too?"

"We've come a long way with medicine, Ahmed. They have treatments for it now."

"So then why didn't they find it earlier in Dad? Prevent it?"

"They were watching him for it. And I pray for Dad every day."

Five times a day, the little digital clock that sat on the kitchen counter played the azaan. Mom said the electronic version was a sorry substitution for the real thing. In the mosque near her house in India, a man would climb into the minaret and sing the prayer call five times a day, inviting everyone to come inside and pray.

Sometimes, she'd say, when the timing was perfect, the church bells, bhajans from the nearby temple, and the azaan would start at the same time. But I knew only our digital version, a little robotic, with a little static. I took it apart once, and Mom was thrilled with my fix. We all pretended not to notice when the static was back the very next day. Five times a day, Mom unfolded her prayer mat to face Mecca and prayed. Dad called himself a once-in-a-while prayer, which meant Fridays at the mosque when he didn't have work.

"So which one is it, Mom? Do they have treatments to cure Dad, or are your prayers supposed to do it?"

"I like to cover all bases."

I wasn't sure which I preferred—the roundabout answers of my dad, or the direct answers of my mom. They each had their disadvantages.

Dad was in the hospital, and it was our last chance to visit him before surgery. I guess those green smoothies worked because he looked great. He was wearing the red hoodie I had given him for his birthday; Prince played in the background; a Gene Hackman movie was on TV. All his favorite things at the same time.

Sara bounced in first, as always, giving him a kiss. "Dad, you look even more handsome in Minnesota than you did in Hawaii."

Dad laughed. "Maybe it's because I look different from most people here."

"Maybe. And your skin isn't even as dark as mine. Anita told me she's in Brownies and wants me to join. She said that maybe since I'm already brown, I wouldn't need a uniform."

They tried to act casual. "So what did you think about that?"

"I'm pretty sure I'll still need a uniform. Anita was jealous because she says the worst part of the meeting is wearing the uniform. She says it's super itchy."

I walked to the window to look outside. This was Dad's second time in this hospital, and my first. I was used to seeing ocean outside the hospital window. I was looking at an almost-empty parking lot with three cars huddled together in the middle.

"You know what I'd really love?" Dad asked, rubbing his belly like a cartoon bear. "I'd love some soup from the cafeteria."

Mom held Sara's hand. "Sara, why don't you come with me? You can get an ice-cream cone." You didn't have to ask her twice.

I got the feeling this was rehearsed.

"So, Ahmed, how're things at school?" Dad asked.

I twisted the rod one way to close the blinds and then

the other way to open them again. "Okay, I guess."

"I know it's a big change, and you must be missing your friends." He pushed the button to lift the head of his bed. "Did you know, Ahmed, that both Mohammed and I were born in this very hospital?"

I twisted the blinds open and light fell like stripes on Dad's face. I twisted them close again.

"The minute I saw you when you were born, when I bent down to say the azaan in your ears to welcome you to the world, I saw my brother in you." He pulled his IV pole behind him as he moved from his bed. "I joked that I had picked the point farthest from Minnesota to get away from the memories, and you brought it all back, right in front of me."

He stood next to me so our shoulders were touching.

"Is this the same hospital where your brother died too?" It sounded angry when I didn't mean it to.

My father, whose answers always took the longest path, answered with a simple "Yes."

"I wish I knew him." I loved having his photo over my locker, like he was looking out for me. I loved knowing his book was the one in my backpack.

"You would have loved him. He would have been the funny uncle who was also your best friend." Dad put his arm around my shoulders. "I wish I had saved more pieces of him. More photos, notes he scribbled and slid under my bedroom door, report cards. Anything and everything."

And that's how we were standing when Mom and Sara came back. Dad's arm around me, me leaning into him, both of us standing at a window with closed blinds.

"You know what this soup needs?" Mom asked. "A little masala powder."

"Mom, NO!" Mom could single-handedly cancel the surgery scheduled for the next day. Her cooking was known to do worse.

CHAPTER
TWENTY-ONE

"I've never been to an apple orchard before," I told Carl the next morning when he picked me up.

He helped his little brother out of his seat and lifted him to the ground. "Ahmed, meet Ben. Ben, meet Ahmed." I put my hand up for a high five, and he jumped up to hit it, totally missing. He had Carl's athletic coordination.

"No one else would come unless I paid them good money. I thought you'd be the only willing sucker."

"Well, thanks for making me feel so popular," I replied.

Carl was a few steps ahead of me but turned to smile. The possibility of a decent friendship rested on whether he recognized sarcasm. He did. Carl out of school was more relaxed than Carl in school.

Dad was going to be in surgery the whole day, and

Mom had arranged for Sara to be at a friend's house. I had a feeling Mom had arranged this trip to the apple orchard too.

Ben chased a mini train he saw across the field; Carl and I took off after him.

"Cawl, go on the twain. Go on the twain," Ben said once we caught up with him. Those little legs could move fast.

"Yeah, Cawl," I added.

The line snaked in front of us, and I couldn't see the front. Families with squirming kids were holding caramel apples, and moms adjusted both kids and apples to capture the perfect selfies. People are always talking about teenagers being addicted to their phones when the real problem is moms.

"You must miss Hawaii. All the pictures I've seen look awesome."

"It's different for sure. I miss my friends, my house. I even miss the centipedes." I kicked away an invisible centipede in the grass in front of me. "But I like it here too." I didn't want Carl to think I was ungrateful for having someone to talk to, a table with room for me at lunchtime, and someone to distract me while Dad was having surgery.

Ben pointed to a guy blowing balloon animals, and

Carl let go of his hand while we kept our spot in line.

"And how're things with you and Jack?" Carl asked.

"Fine."

"Well, if that's what passes as fine where you come from, remind me to never visit." The line moved forward, and Carl moved to the other side of me so he could see Ben.

"Wow, it's that obvious, huh?"

Ben had made it to the front of the balloon line, and we could see him holding his hands wide, trying to explain what he wanted. *Animated*.

"I don't know if it's obvious. I moved here two years ago, and he tried the same crap with me. You've got to let him know you're not going to take it."

Jack picked on Carl with his blue eyes and blond hair? "Wait, he picked on you? I thought he chose me because I looked different."

Ben was hopping on one foot and then the other, like the ground was too hot to plant both. I can't remember being that excited about anything. I'm generally not a hop-on-one-foot sort of guy.

"Nah, that's how he works. He always picks the new kid, the kid without a tribe. That's how I ended up joining Media Club. I was looking for my people." Ben ran back, holding his red balloon sword over his head. "I used to make up stories in my head about him, but the truth is he likes to make others look bad to make himself look better." Ben tugged Carl's arm, pulling him out of line. "I think that may be the official definition of a jerk."

"All done twain," Ben proclaimed.

"But wait, we're almost at the front of the line," I said.

Carl put his hands up in front of him. "That's how it goes, Ahmed. We go where the boss tells us to go."

We spent the next two hours waiting in line for the corn maze but leaving before we got in, waiting in line for face painting and then leaving before we got to the front, and then waiting in line for apple cider and a piece of apple pie. That line I didn't let them quit.

Any day that ends with apple pie is a pretty good day.

CHAPTER
TWENTY-TWO

Dad was doing okay the first day after surgery—as expected, Mom said. She left for the hospital before I woke up, arranging rides for Sara and me to get to school. My ride was Jack's mom.

"Good morning, Mrs. Hanson," I said, but she didn't look my way. She put her index finger in the air asking me to wait. I wasn't sure if I was supposed to wait to get in the car, or just to speak. Jack wasn't going to help me figure it out. I hesitated before getting into the backseat. Neither turned around to acknowledge my presence before backing out of the driveway.

"I can't be there for another two days," Mrs. Hanson said into the phone that was stuck on a magnet on her AC vent. "I need to find someone to watch my son, but I'll be there as soon as I can."

She hung up the phone and looked at me through her rearview mirror, flashing a huge smile. "Why, hello. You must be Ahmed. Glad to meet you."

I waved weakly into the mirror.

"So, what takes you boys into school early today?"

Jack started to explain. "Well, we have this teacher, Mrs. Gaarder, and we get graded on participation, so our group is meeting early to go over our notes."

"Mmm-hmm. What about you, Ahmed? Your mom mentioned you moved from Alaska?"

"Hawaii," I said.

"Mmm-hmm."

"You missed the turn for school, Mom."

"Oh shoot, I meant to turn on the GPS after I was done with the phone call."

"Mrs. Gaarder's class has this competition every year, and no one has ever beaten her. We're going to try this year." I had never heard Jack sound so eager.

Mrs. Hanson punched some things into her phone, one hand on the steering wheel. Mom would not have approved.

"That's nice, dear."

"She makes us read three children's books and talk about them like they're adult books."

The phone rang again, and she answered it, steering

with one hand again. "Okay, okay. I know it's important," she said. "What do you want me to do? Leave him home alone?" There was a long pause while she listened. "Because it's against the law."

Jack didn't try to speak to her for the rest of the ride, and with all her wrong turns we got to school just in time for the bell. Jessica would be furious.

I wanted to say something to Jack. About how my mom gets distracted too. But Mom never ignored me. About how sometimes my mom needed to dump me on someone else. But it wasn't true.

The car pulled away.

"What are you looking at?" I hadn't realized I was looking. And then he growled. Seriously. Like an animal. Not like an animal on the attack, but like a wounded animal. He knocked my backpack to the ground. I picked it up, and feeling sorry for him was replaced with feeling sorry for myself again.

CHAPTER
TWENTY-THREE

With one semi-successful semi-presentation under my belt from the last class, I felt good. We had visited Dad at the hospital the night before. He was weak and didn't open his eyes for us, but I still told him about my first presentation. He would have gotten a kick out of seeing me try.

This must be what the school counselors were hoping I'd feel when they talked about helping me "live up to my potential." I liked it but wasn't convinced it justified the work. Mostly I was relieved my turn to lead the discussion was officially over and someone else could sweat it out.

A few years ago Mom agreed to let me quit piano, but only if I played Beethoven's "Für Elise" perfectly at a recital. I practiced for months, motivated by the possibility of quitting. All that practice paid off, and I didn't make a single mistake. A woman in the front row wiped away tears, and I got the first, and most likely only, standing ovation of my life. Mom hoped the experience would stop me from quitting. Of course, she was wrong. One very intense school counselor whose daughter was also performing at the recital called me a caterpillar making a beautiful change. A *metamorphosis*. Of course, she was wrong too.

I wasn't the metamorphosis type. An overachieving girl, a boy so polite you hated to disappoint him, and fear of physical harm from a bully were not enough to change me into a butterfly.

"Hope everyone's preparing notes and keeping track of the characters," Mrs. Gaarder said, pointing to Carl. "Carl showed me this feature on Connect that makes it easy to keep everything straight. It'll be helpful for the essays. Ask him about it if you have quest-*ions*." She tilted her head toward Carl, who wasn't at all embarrassed about being called out that way. "By the end of the year it's sometimes hard to remember the details. Here's a tip: winning the trophy is in the details. Not that any of you would know." Mrs. Gaarder smiled as she nodded at the trophy. "It hasn't moved from that spot on my desk in all these years, after all." She looked around the room. "The floor is all yours, Carl."

He walked to the front, holding index cards of different colors, back straight and shoulders back, like he was ready for anything. He picked up the trophy and pretended to put it in his pocket. The class laughed, and so did I. I'm pretty sure I looked nothing like that when I was up there. If you looked carefully, you might still see the stain from my puddle of sweat, forever marking the spot where I stood. He shuffled through his index cards, pulled out the yellow ones, and put the rest in his back pocket. For another day, I guess.

"Our group decided to continue the discussion we had last week. When I reviewed the recordings of our group discussions on my phone . . ."

Wait? Did he say recordings? Jessica shot me a dirty look, Ari made a gesture to indicate *next time*, and Jack kicked my seat.

"I noted something," Carl continued, oblivious to the problems he had created for me. "What interested each person in our group was not the themes of the book, or the plot, but the characters. Even more interesting was that, without planning or assigning it, each of us had a different favorite character."

I watched Carl's face as he spoke. The same face that looked like it would cry at the mere mention of an assignment not done looked calm and comfortable, like he belonged there. We weren't different; we were polar opposites.

"We were all reading the same thing," he continued, "but we each rooted for a different person. Sure, the bad guys were still the bad guys, and the good guys were still the good guys, but beyond that we each noticed different things."

Carl paused, waiting for someone to finish coughing.

"I think each of us brings our own background and experiences to what we read, and so we find different favorite characters."

Mrs. Gaarder, who was still standing next to Carl, walked around her desk to sit down. If I hadn't already been seated, I'd have done the same. Carl was in control.

"Everyone feels for Stanley. That one is a no-brainer." He didn't pause, stumble, or stutter. "But we wanted to explain how we related to some of the other characters, especially the ones not as easily likable." It's funny how I thought his voice was rough the first time I heard him, and now it sounded fine. "Each person in our group wanted to speak about who they liked, so we decided to take turns telling you why. Then we can open it up to discussion."

I turned and returned Jessica's dirty look. I gestured to Ari, *next time*. I didn't dare kick Jack's chair.

He put his yellow index cards back in his pocket. He

hadn't looked at them once. He separated the purple ones and a tall, redheaded kid with freckles took them from him. He had arms longer than necessary and was unsure where to put his hands. Finally he kept one on the cards and one thumb hooked to the front pocket of his jeans. "Umm, so my favorite character was, like, Madame Zeroni. I thought she was super smart and should have gotten more play time in the book. I don't believe she really placed a curse on Stanley's family, but I like how she made Stanley's great-great-grandfather carry a piglet every day up the mountain. I think it was smart of her, because as the pig grew bigger, Stanley's great-great-grandfather grew stronger carrying it. He grew stronger without realizing it. Making someone get better without them realizing it is pretty cool. Umm, I guess that's all." Three long steps and he was back in his chair.

Carl moved the pink index cards to the front of his stack. One of those girls who always traveled in a group stood up. I had trouble telling them apart. They wore the same clothes down to the tennis shoes, spoke using the same words and inflection, and ended up looking exactly the same. She was smacking her gum so hard, it was difficult to pay attention to what she said. Brilliant, I thought. Maybe I'd try that next time. "I think Mr. Pendanski, one of the camp counselors, was a great character. He seemed like he genuinely cared about the kids at the camp." Smack, smack. "The kids even called him Mom." Smack, smack. "But he didn't care about the kids any more than the other counselors. I think that was even worse than being mean, because the kids trusted him, and he let them down." Smack, smack. "But I also liked how sneakily evil that was. Yeah, so that's all I really wanted to say." She took a little bow, at which point her friends all giggled. Mrs. Gaarder pointed to the trash can and she spat her gum out before sitting down.

The last person in their group got up, and Carl handed her the white index cards. She looked serious, like she was about to tell us we had only one month to live. "Zero is my favorite," she said. "I think everyone underrated him. He was the best friend out of all of them, the fastest digger, the bravest, and even the smartest. But nobody would know it. I like how he did what needed to be done without bragging or talking about it."

She turned around to look at Carl, who nodded for her to go on.

"I think it was a good lesson to remember that sometimes actions speak louder than words. It's easy to believe what someone tells you, but sometimes it takes longer to believe in someone when they don't." She gave Carl a high five and went back to her seat.

I looked at Carl. She could have been speaking about him. He was the Zero to my Stanley.

CHAPTER
TWENTY-FOUR

Mom and Sara were waiting for me in the garage when I got off the bus. I knocked on the window, and Mom lifted her head off the steering wheel.

"What're you guys doing?" I asked.

Her eyes were both puffy and sunken in. "We were waiting for you to get home to go visit Dad."

"Sounds good to me," I said, opening the front door. The nurses would call it day-five post-op, which means we had sat for four days at Dad's bedside, enjoying the moments he'd be alert long enough to talk to us. We usually went after homework, but before dinner. I didn't ask Mom why the schedule had changed.

We allowed Sara her monologue.

". . . And snack was later than usual because we had an assembly at school, and by then the cheese had gotten really melty and gross."

"Mmm-hmm," Mom said.

". . . And it was Max's turn to have a special reader in class and his great-grandmother came and read us a book. She didn't look like a great-grandmother, even though I don't think she had a single hair that wasn't gray."

"Mmm-hmm."

We had a running commentary all the way to the hospital, but once we parked, Mom interrupted, turning in the seat to face her. "You know how today is the day he was supposed to move out of the ICU?"

I hated the intensive care unit and was excited to have him move out. Walking past all the rooms with the sickest patients made me uncomfortable. Dad wasn't sick like that, was he?

"Well, he had a little setback, so they're keeping him there." She turned to me in the backseat. "They had to put him back on the ventilator. I want you to visit him, but I want you to also be prepared."

Prepared how?

"He's not going to be able to open his eyes, or look at you or talk to you." Mom put one hand on mine and one on Sara's. "But it's only temporary. They don't want his body to work so hard while he's healing."

Dad had been intubated the first night after he came out of surgery. Day zero post-op. But zero meant it didn't count, right? This visit wasn't a little different; it was completely different. We had to wear special yellow gowns and masks before we were allowed to enter, to make sure he didn't catch our germs. Machines beeped, whooshed, and pinged. Dad had a tube in his mouth, and with every whoosh I saw his chest rise and then fall. There were three tall poles like a coat stand with different-sized bags hanging from them. Some were clear, some yellow, and some so precious they were wrapped up, like a baby in a blanket. Dad looked small and weak in his hospital bed, tiny under the tubes and pipes and machines.

Mom's aunt once sent her a special pot from India made of terra-cotta. Mom was convinced it would be the solution to all her biryani-making woes. It came in a crate the size of a kitchen sink. We removed layer after layer of packaging and finally found this tiny pot in a bed of straw in this huge box. That's how Dad looked. Fragile. I stood in the doorway but couldn't get myself to go in. I don't think they needed to worry about him catching germs; he didn't look strong enough to catch a thing.

Mom pulled three chairs to his bed. "I brought you a couple of visitors."

Even Sara was silent. She hesitated at the door and

then took one cautious step toward him.

"You can come closer, honey. I'm sure he'd love to hear your voice." I can't imagine Dad could hear a thing.

"Hi . . . Dad," she whispered, moving one step closer with each word.

I stayed in the doorway, where the pinging-beeping-whooshing got louder in my ears. The room spun and Mom was by my side, her arm over my shoulders as she walked me to my chair.

"Mom . . . is Dad going to be okay?"

"I'm not sure, Ahmed."

CHAPTER
TWENTY-FIVE

Every night when Mom came home, she said Dad had to stay in the ICU for "one more night," and most days when she got back from the hospital Sara was already in bed, and sometimes I was too. When we did see her, she was too tired to talk. When we wanted to visit, Dad "needed his rest." I was hoping Sara hadn't noticed, but she's a smart kid.

Sara sat at the table, finishing her plate of Tuesday night tacos. In black pants and a gray T-shirt with more holes than cloth, she was dressed to match her mood. It was Dad's old T-shirt, the one he was wearing the day they found him, and she had claimed it as her own. The first time we visited Dad in the hospital, I was jealous of Sara. She walked into a room to a dad who hardly recognized her, and still sang him songs, told him about the fight with her best friend, and how her favorite Jolly Rancher flavor was now watermelon and not cherry. I was jealous because she didn't understand how serious it was. The second visit was the same, but I noticed, peeking out under her tutu, Dad's beaten-up gray T-shirt. Since then, whenever Dad got sick, she'd wear it until he was safely back home with us. When I asked her about it, she said, "Well, it brought him back to us once." Today she didn't bother to cover it up. No tutu, no sweatshirt.

"Come on, Sara, let's watch videos of puppies falling asleep." A few years ago, using Sara's old shoebox and the magnifying glass from "my first science kit," I had created my own projector. I could make videos and photos from my phone big enough to cover a wall. On rainy days, we played photos of blue skies and sunshine and spent the day inside, blissfully ignorant of the thunder and lightning. Puppies falling asleep were Sara's favorite.

She didn't bother to reply.

"We could watch one of those ballet videos instead," I said, searching for the most popular ballet videos. "Or you could show me some of your latest dance moves. I haven't seen a twirl for a while." And I realized it was true.

"You never wanted to see me dance before. I'm not stupid, Ahmed. I know you don't want to see me dance now." And again, it was true.

"Of course I do," I pleaded. "I never asked you before because I never had to. In fact, I always had to beg you to stop."

She got up and lifted her foot, ready to do a spin. "Bhaiyya," she said, so I knew she was coming around. She never called me that unless she wanted something from me. "It's so quiet and lonely here, I don't want to dance alone. I need company."

"You want me to dance with you? No way."

"Coooommme oooonn, Bhaiyya, don't you want to dance with your baby sister?" I knew she was playing me, but I also knew she was truly sad. Like me.

I put my hands over my head, pointed my toes, and bent my knees. I kicked my leg out to the side like I had seen her do a million times and heard something come crashing down. It was Mom's favorite pot, an antique she had bought from an old Indian lady who I'm sure was scamming her. It was something ladies spit into, or peed into, or something gross. I'd never understood antiques. I picked it up and looked it over, but couldn't tell if any of the dents were new.

"Let's go to the backyard, Sara. It's not too cold today."

"Yeah, and we can really let loose in the backyard. I'll teach you my best moves. But you know, you can't learn the really hard moves unless you're wearing a tutu."

I gave her my best you-must-be-kidding look. "Listen I'm willing to dance with you, but there's no way I'm wearing a tutu."

"Don't worry about it, Ahmed, I've gone all these months without a twirl, I can make it a few more," she said, and sat back down.

I couldn't tell if she was playing me or not anymore, but I noticed I went from Bhaiyya to Ahmed.

I kept standing, waiting for her to give in and join me, but she didn't.

"Fine, hand me the tutu." I squeezed myself into a purple tutu with glitter at the ends, and she put a tiara on my head. At this point, what did it matter? We went to the backyard, and she taught me to dance. We pirouetted, demi-pointed, and pliéd. I hammed it up for her, and she was all giggles. It felt good.

I was in the cold, tiara crooked on my head, balancing on one leg, other leg outstretched behind me, hands exaggerated into a frame over my head, when I thought I saw a flash. And was that the sound of skateboard wheels?

CHAPTER
TWENTY-SIX

Sara went to sleep in her tutu, so all was well in her head. At least for that night. If only someone could do the same for me.

I took my laptop to bed to finish homework before watching shows. I liked to watch Road Runner cartoons until I fell asleep, rewinding the parts that made Dad laugh. My version of sleeping in a tutu, I guess.

I opened Connect. There would be at least ten messages from Jessica, half begging and the other half yelling at me to prepare for the next class discussion. With 672 friends and followers, Jack's profile was at the top of the list. With three friends and followers, mine was near the bottom. There are 672 students in our school, and I was neither a friend nor a follower of Jack's. The math didn't add up.

Something was different about the photo next to my

name. A few kids had posted photos of themselves. I had laughed at the photo of the girl who had superimposed her face on Arnold Schwarzenegger's body, and been uninspired by the photos of kids holding their favorite iced coffee drinks. Most of the profile photos were blank like mine, just a silhouette of a kid. But today there was a photo. I zoomed in, and it was definitely me. From a few hours ago, in fact. Purple tutu, tilted tiara, stupid grin on my face. I looked like an absolute fool; darn Jack. I tried to log in to delete the picture, but three tries on my password and I was locked out; double darn Jack.

I had barely noticed the change of photo on my profile, and with only three followers and friends, chances were slim that anyone else would see it. I could ignore it, no harm done. But as I scrolled through the list of my classmates, something stood out. All the generic-boy and generic-girl silhouettes were replaced by photos. Every single one. And they were all the same photo. And they were all photos of me. In a tutu. And a tiara. And a stupid grin.

It would take forever to hack into every one of these accounts and change the photos back. I had to hand it to Jack—at least he was creative with his bullying. *Diabolical.* I hated him, but couldn't help but be a little impressed.

I pictured Dad in the hospital, Sara in her gray shirt

with the holes, Mom's exhausted face every night. I couldn't do anything about any of that. It was totally out of my control. But this I could do something about. And I would.

Jack had stepped up his game, so I would have to step up mine. Or at least get in the game. I sneaked into Sara's room, grabbed a couple of things, and shoved them into my backpack.

I thought about what that guy said in English class. Stanley's great-great-grandfather had gotten stronger by carrying that pig up the hill every day. As the pig grew bigger, he got stronger.

Jack was my pig.

CHAPTER
TWENTY-SEVEN

Once, while waiting at the dentist's office, I had read about Hollywood stars getting colonics. I knew the colon was the large intestine, and from the article I understood that it was a cleanse of some sort, but Mom had to explain the details. She laughed and added, "Some people will stick their money anywhere." I had no desire, intention, or plan to have someone put coffee up my butt, but I imagine the feeling they were hoping for was exactly what I felt that morning. Like someone had given me permission to change the things I could change. That someone was me.

I felt fresh, renewed, and ready to take on whatever came my way. I can handle carrying the pig, I told myself. The first hole is the hardest, I told myself.

Maybe Jack sensed it, because he left me alone. He

left me alone while we waited for the bus, while we were on the bus, and while we got off the bus. Was it guilt? Remorse?

"Hey, Ahmed," Jack called from behind me, "wait up a sec." His voice was sweet and slippery. Remorse was too strong an emotion for Jack. Of course he had one of his buddies with him, silent but present.

"I have this slight problem, Ahmed, and I was hoping you could help," he said. He almost sounded sincere.

"Sure, Jack, what's up?" I played it cool, like I had no idea what he was talking about. Like we were friends who had conversations all the time. Like my heart didn't pound and my palms didn't sweat when I saw him.

"Well, I have something great, but I'm not sure how to use it well. I'm afraid I should have saved it for a more opportune moment," he replied. His friend laughed.

I heard what he was saying, but all I could think was opportune. Jack used the word *opportune*? I tightened my grip on the strap of my backpack.

"Umm . . . what's this thing you're talking about, Jack?"

"Well, it's this perfect little thing. It's got romance. It's got adventure. Wait, you know how they say a picture is worth a thousand words? Maybe it's easier for me to show you."

He took a stack of papers from his friend and handed me a folded sheet. I stopped walking to open it. If there was any doubt about Jack being the one who posted the photo, there wasn't now. I was looking straight at myself. He thumbed through a stack of papers with my face printed on every one. "You can have that copy. I have plenty more."

Any other day I would have frozen, not knowing how to respond. Today, however, I was prepared and unbeatable. Colonic unbeatable. "You keep it, Jack. I've got that memory locked away right here," I told him as I handed it back and pointed to my heart. "You may want to consider a better-quality printer next time, though." I walked away, but not before I saw the look of complete confusion on Jack's face. *Perplexed*.

By the end of first hour, there was a photo taped to my locker, and looking down the hall I saw my photo everywhere. On lockers, water fountains, bulletin boards, classroom doors. People who didn't know me were pulling my face off their lockers and having a good laugh.

Mrs. Gaarder found me in the hall. She had one of my photos in her hand. "So, Ahmed, you want to talk about this? Are you okay?"

I took the photo from her and held it by my face, re-creating the goofy smile to show her I could laugh this off. "Don't I look okay?" I asked.

"You're sure?"

"Yup." I was sure.

By lunch there wasn't a kid in school who hadn't seen the photo. But just in case, Jack had been to the lunchroom before me and taped a photo on every table. I had to hand it to him: he was very thorough.

As I moved down the lunch line, I was very popular that day.

"Ballerina, keep the line moving."

"Hey, what's the difference between a plié and a pirouette?"

"Did you forget your tutu at home?"

It was the last day of school before Thanksgiving break. I had two choices. The first was to make it through the day by ignoring the photos and comments. By the time everyone came back from break, it would be long forgotten. Jack could then find some other way to torture me. And then another. And then another. I chose option two.

I left my tray on the table and headed to the front of the cafeteria. In my backpack was the brown paper bag with the things I had collected from Sara's room. I balanced the tiara on my head. For the second time in as many days, I pushed my legs through the tutu. No one noticed. I felt a wave of nausea like that day in elementary school when we stood outside in the heat and I had ignored everyone's advice to drink more water. Right before I passed out. I steadied myself before re-creating the pose from the photo as best I could. Like those guys who painted themselves like statues, I stood absolutely still.

I didn't know what to expect. A couple of eighth grad-ers stopped to look at me, but then kept going. A girl walked past and laughed. One boy shrugged. I contin-ued to stand there, the unexpected ballerina.

Jessica stood in front of me, empty tray in hand. "Ahmed Aziz, what the heck are you doing?"

"I'm pulling a Jessica."

"Huh?"

"You must have seen the photos everywhere, right? I thought I'd have people laugh with me instead of at me."

"And that's a Jessica?"

"Definitely."

She looked pleased. "Okay, Ahmed. I like what you're doing here." She stepped up on the small stage, put her tray down in front of her, and stood next to me. She stepped her leg behind her and curved her hands over her head, holding the same pose as me.

"What're you doing?" I asked.

"What does it look like? Don't forget the dumb look

you had on your face in the photo," she said as she did her best imitation of me. And the two of us stood next to each other, not moving or speaking. My stomach growled.

Without asking what we were doing, Carl struck the same pose. Ari rolled his wheelchair to the side of the stage and did the same. One by one, it felt like every single person in the cafeteria joined us, not asking why or what. Maybe they assumed it was one of those internet challenges; maybe they didn't care. Only Jack was left sitting at a table in the far corner.

When the bell rang, we all broke into laughter and everyone went to class. Cacophony again. Except this time, I was part of it.

Jessica was at my side and gave me a friendly punch on my shoulder. "You see, Ahmed, one person standing in a tutu for no reason is pointless. Everyone standing at the front—now that's a movement. You might want to call it a Jessica."

CHAPTER
TWENTY-EIGHT

Thanksgiving was always Dad's favorite holiday because it reminded him of celebrating Eid with his parents. Both holidays are about food, friends, and family. The three of us sat around the table, the tandoori turkey barely touched. An auntie had dropped off the whole Thanksgiving meal, and nothing tasted like I remembered. I pushed the mashed potatoes around my plate before calling it quits and going to bed.

Dad was still in the ICU. Every day he looked smaller and the machines around him looked bigger, like he was disappearing. So nothing tasted good.

I woke up tired, and my head ached, like I hadn't slept the whole night. The house was strangely still for eleven o'clock in the morning.

"Mom?" I yelled to no one. "Sara?" My voice echoed

in the quiet. *Reverberated.*

I fiddled with the charger and waited impatiently for my phone to come to life. Unread texts rolled in.

> **Mom (11:01 p.m.):** *Ahmed, got a message from the hospital. I'm going to see Dad. Not waking the two of you. Should be back soon.*
>
> **Mom (1:15 a.m.):** *Still at the hospital. Everything is OK.*
>
> **Unknown number (2:12 a.m.):** *Ahmed, this is Mrs. Gaarder. I wanted you to have my number in case you need anything. Don't hesitate to call me any time.*
>
> **Mom (5:18 a.m.):** *On my way home.*
>
> **Mom (8:04 a.m.):** *I'll let you sleep. Going back to the hospital. Dropping Sara at a friend's house.*
>
> **Unknown number (9:20 a.m.):** *Mrs. Gaarder again. Call me when you're ready, and I'll take you to the hospital.*
>
> **Me (11:15 a.m.):** *I'm ready Mrs. Gaarder*

Neither of us needed directions to the ICU. Mrs. Gaarder stopped at the nurse's station, her questions answered with nods and whispers.

"The doctors are working with your father right now. They'll let your mom know we're here."

The elevator doors opened, releasing men and women

hurrying down the hall in scrubs and clogs, untied masks hanging around their necks like tiny bibs.

Dad was in Room 310. Room 310 was in the hallway they were hurrying through.

It didn't matter that I had never been in this waiting room; I assumed my position. Waiting rooms everywhere were the same. I wondered if there was a kid in a hospital waiting room in Lithuania looking at a basket of children's books with covers pulled off and a half-finished puzzle on the table. Mom came in and gave me a weak smile. There was a coffee stain on the front of her shirt, and one sock fell limp around her ankle. She hugged me so tight my chest hurt.

"Janet, thanks for bringing him." They hugged, and it felt strange to see these two parts of my life collide.

We sat around the puzzle of an English countryside.

"Code Blue, Room 310 ICU. Repeat, Code Blue, Room 310 ICU," was announced over the PA system. Mom wrapped her hand around mine. I knew what and who they were talking about. My father's heart must have stopped. It felt like mine had as well.

Maybe I hadn't heard it right; maybe it wasn't Dad's room. There was something eerie about the silence that followed the echoing of the PA announcement, and I didn't want to break it to ask the question. The

PA crackled again.

"Code Blue, Room 310 ICU. Repeat, Code Blue, Room 310 ICU."

Question answered. Mom tightened her grip.

"Janet, Sara needs to be picked up, but do you mind taking her home? I'll let you know when I need you to bring her here," Mom whispered.

Mrs. Gaarder got up, hesitated, but moved to the door. She came back and crouched down to put one hand on Mom's shoulder and one on mine, hugging us like we were one person. Her eyes glistened, and she opened her mouth but said nothing. She squeezed my shoulder before she left.

I counted the puzzle pieces on the table in front of me, noticing a corner piece I could place, but not bothering to. I counted to eight hundred before a doctor walked in; his graying hair peeked out of his surgical cap, and his eyebrows needed a trim. He sat down in Mrs. Gaarder's chair.

"Well, Mrs. Aziz, we've got him stabilized again. His heart is beating, but we are helping him with everything else. He's on medication to keep his blood pressure up, and he's still on the machine to keep him breathing." A granola bar stuck out of his pocket. I thought about him talking to us and then going to eat his granola bar. It didn't seem fair. "The next twenty-four hours are going to be crucial. We're supporting him in every way possible, but he's going to have to do the rest." He leaned over and put his hand on Mom's. It was oats and nuts. But it was an awkward movement, and he took his hand back with a jerk. Mom didn't notice.

"Give them a few minutes to clean up, and then you can see him." He turned around when he got to the door. "He seems like a fighter, Mrs. Aziz. Let's hope for the best."

Mom nodded.

"I'm going to drop you home, Ahmed."

"No, Mom, I'm going to stay here with you. I need to."

She looked at her feet, straightened her sock, dusted off her shirt, and buttoned her sweater to cover the stain. Her voice was more her own. "Janet will be home with Sara. I need you to be there for her. I'll come back to the hospital and come home first thing in the morning."

I stood up to leave. "Can I see Dad before I go?"

"Why don't we plan for you to see him tomorrow, Ahmed?"

A piano tune played over the PA, announcing the birth of a baby. The tune was longer than usual. Twins.

"But what if by tomorrow he's—"

"You can see him tomorrow morning, Ahmed."

We drove home, neither of us speaking, missing Sara's uninterrupted chatter. Mom pulled into our driveway next to Mrs. Gaarder's car.

"Please tell Janet I had to rush back to the hospital and tell her thank you again. And of course, Ahmed, use your manners."

Yup, Mom was back.

Sara was upstairs, and Mrs. Gaarder was sitting in the purple chair holding a magazine. I had seen her in the strangest of places. When I woke up that morning if you had told me I would see my English teacher hugging my mom in the ICU and come home to see her in our favorite chair, I would have called you a liar.

I stood there, half of me in the dark of the mudroom and half of me in the light of the kitchen, feeling awkward and unsure in my own home.

"Come in, Ahmed. You must be hungry." A brown bag with grease stains sat on the counter. "There's tons of Indian food in the fridge that everyone's been dropping off, but Sara and I bought burgers and fries. They're on the counter if you want some."

I kept standing there. Half of me wanting to go in and half of me wanting to stay still.

She rubbed her hand along the arms of the purple

chair. "You know, I was with your dad when he got this chair."

I stepped inside.

"You were?" I asked.

"Yes, I was. Come in, I'll tell you all about it."

And I did, because all of me needed to.

CHAPTER
TWENTY-NINE

Mrs. Gaarder opened a few cabinets before she found a plate. She placed the burger in the middle before tilting the pack of fries so they fell like an arch around it.

"So many of my high school memories have your dad in them," she said.

"Yup, a long, long time ago."

She took a french fry off my plate and dipped it in ketchup, and it didn't feel strange.

"Hey, one *long* would have been enough. But you're right, it was a while ago. Your dad and I became good friends eventually. But you know your uncle and I were friends first. Your dad and I only got to know each other after your uncle . . ."

"Died." I was always having to fill in that word for

others. "I didn't know that."

"Mohammed and I were best friends. From the first day of kindergarten, when both of us fought over a book about transistor radios."

She wrapped her arms to hug herself. "I didn't care one bit about transistor radios, but I didn't like him saying girls knew nothing about radios. So we fought over it." I moved her story along when she went quiet.

"My uncle liked books?" Maybe we weren't as similar as Dad made it sound.

She laughed out loud. "Oh, absolutely not. I loved books. He hated them. He loved radios, mechanical things, taking things apart, putting them back together."

My uncle was a techie. Like me.

"So how did you and Dad end up being friends?"

"Well"—she rubbed one thumb with the other in circles—"after your uncle . . . died"—she said the word before I had to—"your dad searched me out. Your dad wanted someone to talk to about his brother. He wanted to talk about him like he was alive, not as a tragedy."

She stole another fry from my plate.

"We spent so much time together, people even thought we were dating." I scrunched my face in disgust, and Mrs. Gaarder laughed. "That's how we felt about it too. Your dad and I became friends to keep your uncle's memory alive, and that's what we've done ever since."

I licked the corner of my mouth where salt had collected and took a sip of soda. "So, what's the story with the purple chair?"

"Have you heard of the musician Prince? I don't know what's popular with kids these days, but he was the greatest. He was from here, you know." Pointing outside, like he lived across the street. "There was a place downtown where he liked to play. He'd show up without warning, and catching one of those shows felt like the point of our entire existence."

She tore off a paper towel, picked up my glass, and wiped away the ring of condensation.

"You had to know a guy who knew a guy to get info about when Prince would be showing up. Your dad was my guy."

I put a couple of fries in the middle of my burger before taking the next bite.

Mrs. Gaarder laughed. "I remember your uncle used to do that too. Anyway, one night your dad heard that Prince was going to be playing and called to tell me. It was a school night and a group of us sneaked out . . . Wait, maybe I shouldn't be telling you this."

"Too late now, Mrs. Gaarder," I said, my words slurred by my mouthful of french fry burger.

"I guess so. Well, we sneaked out and waited outside that club for hours. It was February, so much colder than it is now, if you can imagine that, and without all your fancy-technology type coats to keep us warm, and no heating in his car. We waited there until midnight, but no one showed up."

Mrs. Gaarder took an orange from the fruit bowl and peeled it in one unbroken swirl.

"We were about to give up when your dad saw that big purple chair in the alley behind the club. He got it in his head that it was Prince's. Because it was purple." She smiled to herself, lost for a moment in her memory. "He convinced us that it must have been abandoned, and we deserved it for waiting so long in the cold." She leaned back in her stool, feet not touching the floor. "Well, as you know, it's a pretty big chair. He had a pretty small car. It took us an hour to get it tied to the top of his car using pieces of rope we found in the trash can in the alley." She pulled white threads off her slice of orange, arranging the discarded threads into small piles on the counter in front of her. "I remember we had to lean out the window on both sides and hold it in place the whole time we rode back. In February. He was worried we'd lose the chair, but we're lucky we didn't lose a finger. But we did it."

She walked back to the chair, stroking its arm like an old friend before sitting down. "And that, Ahmed, is how you got that purple chair."

Something about that story made me want to cry.

One after another, she told me stories of Dad and my uncle, and I don't remember falling asleep, but when I woke up Mom had replaced Mrs. Gaarder in the purple chair. I sat up straight, fully awake. "Is Dad . . . okay?" I couldn't get myself to use a different word.

She nodded. "He is, for now."

BOOK
TWO

CHAPTER
THIRTY

According to the calendar on my phone, the first day of winter hadn't formally arrived. Apparently Minnesota isn't big on formality, because winter was most definitely here. I ran inside to switch from sweatshirt to my winter jacket, leaving the price tags in the bowl of keys at the front door. There was something wet on my nose, and I wiped it away. I felt it again on the back of my neck and turned around to see if Jack was playing a prank on me. He wasn't. I pulled the hood over my head, the fuzzy lining warm against my cheek.

"Look who thinks they're in Siberia." Jack was wearing a sweatshirt and shorts.

The wetness touched my hand, and I looked around again.

"Umm . . . it's snowing, dude," said Sofie, the girl with

the big feet. "Haven't you ever seen snow?"

In kindergarten we cut snowflakes out of paper and taped them to our classroom windows, but they faded and turned yellow by the time we returned from winter break. Even fake snow couldn't survive in Hawaii. These snowflakes were nothing like those. They were cool and light, and my breath melted them before they could land on my tongue. Big, fat, juicy snowflakes. Watching each flake float before it landed made it hard to feel sorry for myself. I watched the green grass and the black road and the brown roofs all turn white, but each step I took left black footprint–shaped destruction, and I was back to thinking about my dad and feeling sorry for myself.

I dragged myself around all morning, avoiding eye contact and conversation. By lunchtime I felt like I had an angry black cloud drawn over my head. Carl noticed, of course. He brought up Hawaii, sunshine, and swimming pools. *It's not winter that's bugging me*, I wanted to yell at him. Instead I pulled out my copy of *From the Mixed-Up Files of Mrs. Basil E. Frankweiler* to shut him out. I was halfway through the book but still hadn't gotten into it. Unlike Stanley from *Holes*, the main character in this book, Claudia, seemed like a brat. She had a father who was not in the ICU and a school where no one picked on her, but she ran away from home. I couldn't understand her. If I met her, I would have punched her. Well, probably not. But she would have deserved it.

"Carl, what the heck is Claudia's problem anyway?"

"What do you mean?"

"Why do you think she ran away?"

"I don't know. I think she was looking for something." That sounded dumb. It's perfectly easy to search for something without running away, in the comfort of your bedroom, with a good meal in your belly. In fact, it's preferable. "Looking for what, do you think?"

"I don't think she knew, but my theory is that she was looking for the truth," Carl said. "Ahmed, do your own homework." My turn leading the discussion was thankfully over, but Jessica had sent me multiple threatening messages reminding me to increase my participation.

Someone threw a stack of newspapers on the middle of our table. It was the school paper. The front page covered the last game and school lunches. From Hawaii to Minnesota, there was a common thread to what fascinated us.

The Cedar Valley Chatter
A school newspaper since 1927

There was no bragging or exaggeration; they called it

Minnesota nice. Any other paper would have said "best newspaper around" or "best school around." But no, it was "a" school newspaper. Since 1927.

Jack pressed a finger on the edge of my tray as he passed by, tipping it over. Cake smashed, spaghetti splattered, chocolate milk pooled. Another color added to my tennis shoes.

"Hey," Carl shouted at Jack, "stop being such a jerk."

I felt too tired to even wish I had a comeback.

I flipped the tray over and scooped the spaghetti in. Carl scraped the cake in with his spoon. I covered the milk with my napkin.

"Why do you let him do that?" Carl asked.

I didn't bother wiping my shoes.

"What's the point, Carl?"

Carl was crouched over the cake, spoon still in hand. "What's the point? What's the point? The point, my friend, is to save the innocent." He stood up, put one leg on the bench, the frosting-covered spoon in front of him like a microphone. "I have witnessed an atrocity today," Carl said in a deep, newscaster voice. "Innocent cake, chocolate milk that never hurt a fly, spaghetti limp with exhaustion. They never stood a chance. And what do the privileged say—the men and women given the resources and intelligence to fight? Do they rally in the face of this injustice? Do they bring the troops together with the singular hope of saving the voiceless? No, ladies and gentlemen, they ask today only one question. What. Is. The. Point?"

No one laughed or cheered or noticed. It was Carl being Carl. I fake clapped, and he bowed. I felt like smushed cake. I hadn't done anything to deserve the way Jack put me down, but I guess I also hadn't done anything to deserve the way Carl lifted me up.

I had no appetite. I left the Chatter behind and headed to class.

Mrs. Gaarder was already at her desk, red pen in hand, making kids' lives miserable one test at a time. I tried to back out quietly before she saw me, but I was too slow.

"Ahmed," she called, pulling me back in. "I was about to call your mother. How's your dad doing?"

"Nothing much has changed in the last couple of weeks." Mom kept telling us we were lucky he wasn't getting worse. Somehow I didn't feel very lucky.

If I sat down, I was stuck until class started. If I hung out at the door, I still had a chance.

"Come sit down." Too slow again. I zoned out while she talked about how she was there for me and asked me to let her know if there was anything she could do. There was nothing anyone could do. I focused my attention on rolling the newspaper on my lap into a tight tube.

"You know, I started that newspaper," she said.

I unrolled the paper and tried to smooth it out. "You did?" I asked, eager to talk about anything but my dad.

"Wow, Ahmed. 1927. How old do you think I am? But I did write for the paper all the years I was here," she said.

She took the paper from me and opened it up, covering her table. "I used to be a page-two person. That was the page that covered world news. Probably the least-read section of the entire paper." The pages crinkled as she turned them. "I recruited all my friends to write for the paper. All of them."

The class trickled in. I wanted to move seats before the bell rang. It was bad enough being the new kid without being the new kid who was friends with the teacher.

"Hey, Mrs. Gaarder, how're you doing?" Carl asked. Carl had no such worries.

"Doing well, Carl. Thank you so much for asking," she answered. "Ahmed needs to navigate the library to do some research. Do you mind helping him sometime?"

I did? She folded the newspaper and held it out for me. "Some very specific research," she added.

CHAPTER
THIRTY-ONE

I met Carl at the library after school, standing in front of the encyclopedias, not knowing where to start. *Dawdling.* I didn't know how to tell Carl what I was looking for, because I didn't know what I was looking for.

"I'll be right back." Carl dug through his backpack. "I have to return a book."

I moved to the biographies and thumbed through a book about Ruth Bader Ginsburg. Never heard of her, but people will write books about anyone. E. L. Konigsburg, that name I knew. I looked at the back flap. "Did you know," it said, "that Konigsburg was inspired to write her most famous book when she saw a kernel of popcorn on a chair behind a velvet rope?" Who cared? I put Konigsburg and her popcorn fame back on the shelf.

"What are we looking for today?" Carl asked.

I was pretty sure Mrs. Gaarder wanted me to look through school newspapers. That's all I was sure of. "I don't know. How do I look through old school newspapers?"

"How old are we talking?" Carl asked.

That's one of the things I liked about Carl. He didn't ask, why? Or what? Or when? He was just there.

"About thirty or forty years old."

"Oh, that's easy. If you were looking for something older than that, we'd have to go to a different building. Papers from fifty years ago are still here, though. You're lucky."

First time I'd been lucky in the last six months, for sure.

He took me to a corner of the library tucked away in the far end. There were rows of books of the same height and thickness. Some were older and bound in leather, and some were covered in plastic. There were no markings along the binding, and when I pulled one down there were no words on the front cover.

"There you go," he said. "All the newspapers for the past fifty years."

"So, where's the index? How's it organized?" I asked.

"That's where your luck runs out. The person in

charge of binding them together didn't put them in any particular order. Nobody put a date or index on that thing." Carl stepped to the side and out of the way. "I tried to find out how the school got its name. I gave up before I lost my sanity. They aren't even in chronological order."

I rubbed the bindings, releasing a puff of dust. I wiped my hand on my jeans and coughed.

"Hey, you're like Claudia," Carl said, walking down the aisle and dragging his finger along the books, "looking for something in *The Mixed-Up Files*."

And like Claudia, I was looking for answers without knowing the question. Maybe I wouldn't punch her in the face after all.

CHAPTER
THIRTY-TWO

Mom microwaved idlis and put them on a plate in front of me, another early morning for me.

"Want to visit Dad after school today?" she asked. I was turning the idlis in my plate like a DJ and stopped them mid-spin.

"I'll come," answered Sara without hesitating, her idlis hidden under a mountain of sugar.

I dipped mine in chutney. "Maybe." Dad was still in the ICU and still intubated, and I still wasn't excited about sitting by his bedside when he couldn't hear or see us. Also, I needed more time in the library. Words I never thought I'd say.

"Think about it," replied Mom. "I'm sure he'd really like to have you there."

Most days we had to pick Jack up as well. My preference

was that he not talk to me and I not talk to him. I had learned to avoid walking with him by giving him a head start while I adjusted my jacket, or fiddled with the car door, or looked for something in my bag.

Mom kept trying to get a conversation going.

"You like tacos? Ahmed loves tacos."

"Oh, nice," Jack replied. Everyone likes tacos, Mom.

"You like to sleep in late? Ahmed loves to sleep in late."

"Oh, nice," Jack replied. Everyone likes to sleep in, Mom.

Jack was always polite and would always respond. Except one time.

"Ahmed and I have talked about inviting you for dinner. Come by any time you get lonely."

Whoa, Ahmed and she had never talked about it. One night, she mentioned Jack must be lonely and suggested we invite him. I hadn't agreed.

To this, Jack didn't respond. He got very quiet in the backseat, and Mom eventually put us out of our misery by turning on the music.

I spent enough time tying my shoes to allow Jack to be a few steps ahead. When he turned around, his face was red.

"I like being alone at home."

"Listen, Jack, I never even said anything. I don't know what she was talking—"

"I feel so sorry for you, Ahmed. I can't imagine having to live your life," he said before walking ahead of me into the building.

I was the first to arrive in the cafeteria, not sure where Jack was. I waited, notebook open, ready to go. Jessica was the next to arrive. "Whoa, look who's getting serious," she said. "Does this mean you've read the book this time?"

"Read it? I could have written it."

"Prove it."

"What? Like a book report?"

"Yup. Like a book report."

"Well, it's the story of a family who lives in the suburbs of New York. Claudia, who's twelve years old, convinces her nine-year-old brother to run away to Manhattan, where they hide in the Metropolitan Museum of Art."

"Well, that proves you read the first couple of chapters."

I held my hand up, letting her know I had more. "There's a mystery behind a Michelangelo statue in the museum. Claudia feels she will be ready to go home when she solves it. The solution to their mystery is found in the very strangely organized filing system of Mrs. Frankweiler."

"Way to read the jacket cover, Aziz," Jessica said.

Ari and Jack came in together. "Geez, chill out, Jessica," Ari said. "You're going to get an ulcer before you're twenty."

The decorating committee was there early, dragging boxes and ladders. They started at the other end of the cafeteria, taking down construction-paper autumn leaves and cardboard-cutout cornucopias. In case the foot of snow outside wasn't enough reminder that fall was over.

"Nice job!" Ari yelled to one of the decorators.

"Thanks!" she yelled back.

As usual, I didn't know what they were talking about. "For what?" I asked.

"Didn't you see her on Morning Report yesterday? She was Student of the Month. She collected more coats and blankets to give away this winter than anyone else."

"I was supposed to be Student of the Month—" Jack started to say.

"For what?" Jessica interrupted with a laugh.

Jack ignored her laugh. "For having the most followers on Connect."

"Geez, I didn't realize they were so desperate." She got us back to business. "Why don't we get started?"

"Sounds good to me," Ari answered. "This time, I think we should focus on the different characters."

"I know. I know. I'll take notes," I said. I drew columns

and rows in my notebook. "I'll keep track of every pearl of wisdom you drop, Jessica."

"I'm liking you more and more, Ahmed. But you need to raise your hand a little more in class. Did you see the board? We're an inch behind Carl's team." As soon as Mrs. Gaarder had unveiled the scores after we'd finished *Holes*, I knew Jessica would get even pushier. I didn't think that was possible.

"The nice thing about this book is that there are only three main characters," she continued. "There's Claudia, her brother Jaime, and Mrs. Frankweiler. If all of us share a couple of ideas about each, maybe Ahmed can put together some good notes. I'll start."

"Of course," Ari said with a smile. "We wouldn't have it any other way."

The ladder fell, rattling through the cafeteria. Like a car's wiper across a windshield, the decorating committee had cleared the leaves off the far corner, wiping fall clean.

"Well, I really like Claudia. I love how she knows what she wants and goes for it," Jessica said.

"I don't know," Jack said, "I think Claudia is kind of weird. She has everything she could want and still runs away from home. I don't get it."

I agreed with Jack but would never admit it. First I admired the creativity of his bullying, and now I was agreeing with his thoughts on this book. What was next? Inviting him home after school to play video games and drink hot chocolate?

"I didn't really like Claudia either," I said, "but I did like the way she took off on this adventure without knowing exactly what she was going to do. That took guts. She was looking for something and was willing to do anything to find it." Sure, I stole a little from Carl, but that didn't make it less true or less mine.

Like most days, Jessica had the most to say, and Ari waited for a space to open up before he spoke. "Anything to add, Ari?"

"Honestly, I didn't like Claudia either. She is too bossy for me, but I like how she included Jaime in things, like being in charge of the money. She learned to let him be an important part. Jessica, you see how that works? Need to take notes?"

She ignored him.

I looked at my notes. All of us had read the same book, but we each saw Claudia in different ways. That was kind of cool.

"Did you get that, Ahmed?" Jessica asked.

"Umm, what did you say, Claudia—I mean, Jessica?" Which made Ari laugh.

"I said I can feel that trophy in my hands already."

I looked at my notes. I had two full pages.

"What's the deal with that trophy? I could get each of you one for a couple of dollars if you wanted."

Ari started to pack his things up. "You'll get it when you've been here a little longer. Beating Mrs. Gaarder would be legendary. It would make the team who beat her legendary."

The back wall was completely cleared, and the decorating committee began putting things up. There were snowmen and tinsel and menorahs and a Christmas tree and my kindergarten snowflakes. I was not expecting any crescents or stars for Eid. Mom suggested I join the committee if I cared about having Eid decorations, about being represented, as she put it. Representation would be nice, but I didn't care enough to be a joiner.

"Okay, I think we've got enough," Jessica said. "The bell is going to ring soon anyway. Jack, you were pretty quiet today."

Jack turned to me instead of Jessica. "Yeah, I'm working on something, and it's taking a lot of my attention right now." While the others were busy putting chairs back, Jack knocked my notebook to the floor.

Thanks a lot, Mom.

I guess we weren't ready for hot chocolate and video games.

CHAPTER
THIRTY-THREE

After school, searching through old newspapers, I really felt like Claudia. And like Claudia, I didn't know what I was looking for, but I needed to find it.

I asked Mrs. Gaarder more than once.

"You'll know it when you see it," she answered.

I looked through everything, gathering utterly useless information along the way. I knew why the mascot was changed: cultural sensitivity. I knew the school play performed in 1982: *Alice in Wonderland*. I found the article Carl wanted about how the school got its name: a vote at a boring city council meeting. What I didn't find was what I was looking for: what Mrs. Gaarder was hoping I'd find.

I skimmed for pictures and dates remotely related to my family, assuming that's what she wanted me to find.

I glanced over winners of science fairs, lists of colleges chosen by seniors, and comic strips poorly drawn and barely decipherable. What made me stop to read every time, though, was the advice column. It was written to "Dear Grumpy Old Man," and I must have the soul of a grumpy old man, because I loved his advice.

> *Dear Grumpy Old Man,*
> *My friends all have nicknames for each other. They nicknamed me Chubby. I pretended to laugh when they told me, but I don't think it's funny.*
> *Sincerely,*
> *Enough*
>
> *Dear Enough,*
> *Sticks and stones may break my bones, but names will never hurt me. That's the dumbest thing anyone ever told me.*
> *You know the smartest thing anyone ever told me? It was Eleanor Roosevelt. She said no one can make you feel bad without your permission. Or something like that. When my wife told me not to wear my pants so high, I told her Eleanor Roosevelt told me I could wear my pants anyway I pleased.*
> *Maybe your friends don't know how you feel? Tell*

them. And if they don't listen, maybe it's time for you to find new friends.

Sincerely,

Grumpy Old Man

Dear Grumpy Old Man,

My friend had a party and didn't invite me. She said she forgot and keeps apologizing, but I don't think I can forgive her. Maybe I'll have a party and forget to invite her. Then she'd understand how I feel.

Sincerely,

Angry

Dear Angry,

I was eating my dinner at 4 p.m. like I always do, the Early Bird Special, you know? I got a great fortune in my cookie. It said, "Before you embark on a journey of revenge, you'd better dig two graves." I don't have the energy to look for my shovel, let alone dig two graves, do you?

Your friend was wrong, and I'm glad she said sorry. Sometimes it's hard to forgive someone, but sitting there stewing in your own anger only gets in the way of your own happiness.

At my shuffleboard game yesterday someone "accidentally" moved my puck, and I lost the game. I

wanted to clock him in the face, but I didn't.
Sincerely,
Grumpy Old Man

Dear Grumpy Old Man,
A friend of mine struggles with fitting in. I keep telling him to just be himself, but he prefers to pretend he's something he's not—just to fit in. Any advice for him?
Signed,
Awkward

Dear Awkward,
You're asking "for a friend"? Right? Wink, wink.
Some old fart once said, "Be yourself, because everyone else is taken." Stay true to who you are. You be you. But I've got to agree with "your friend" on this one, and I don't like agreeing with anyone. Pretend to laugh about something, and sometimes you'll find it funny. Pretend to cry about something, and sometimes you'll find it sad. For the little things, it's okay to pretend.
Sincerely,
Grumpy Old Man

That was advice I knew well, because I had been getting that same advice all my life. Fake it till you make it.

I tried to flip through one of the leather-bound volumes,

but the pages stuck together. I separated them, and a grainy photo at the bottom caught my eye. He was much younger, a little thinner, and he had more hair, but I could have recognized those eyebrows and that smile anywhere. It was my father. His hand was casually slung over someone's shoulders. No one else in the photo was aware their picture was being taken, but not my father. He was smirking straight at the camera. He was casual and happy, and somehow light. So different from his brother. So different from me. "Bill, Jacob, and friends taking a break during SATs," read the caption under the photo.

When Dad ate curry with a fork and knife instead of with his hands, or when he complained about Indians never being on time getting somewhere, Mom teased him by calling him Bill. A lifetime ago, Dad was Bill instead of Bilal. His American name, he joked. Only Bill and Jacob were named in the caption. Usually I was the unnamed kid in the picture. *Unacknowledged.*

I didn't notice Carl standing next to me.

"You're still in the library?" he asked. "Must be important."

"Hey, Carl, look at this. It's a picture of my dad."

"Whoa. I didn't know he went here. He reminds me of you."

I always knew Carl was pretty cool.

CHAPTER
THIRTY-FOUR

"Today," Mrs. Gaarder started, "we begin my absolute favorite book, *From the Mixed-Up Files of Mrs. Basil E. Frankweiler*. Are you *ready*?" she asked as she called on someone at the other end of the room. It didn't matter who it was, as long as it wasn't me.

I recognized him from our bus. I had nicknamed him "cool guy." I'm observant but not creative. In direct contrast to me, he was always comfortable, above all the middle school drama. He was passing the time with us lesser mortals until he was in his own cool apartment in his own cool city, doing his own cool thing, like designing skateboards or managing rappers.

"The theme our group chose today for discussion is family," he said.

I looked over my notes. Family wasn't a topic we had

discussed in our group.

"Family kept popping up throughout the book. Claudia ran away from home but chose to take her brother with her. We found it interesting that she was running away from her family, but she chose to take family with her."

He pushed his hands into his sweatshirt pockets and blew away hair that had fallen across his eyes.

"I wonder if the author is trying to tell us we can never run away from family. That we always take it with us."

No wonder it wasn't in my notes. It wasn't in my notes because it didn't make sense. I don't think the author was trying to say anything that deep. I think the story would have been boring with one kid roaming around a museum, so Claudia took her brother. Ridiculous. I raised my hand, and cool guy called on me. "I don't think it was about family at all. I think it was about Claudia and her search for the truth. After all, the book only had three characters, and one of them wasn't even family."

Cool guy uncrossed his legs and ran his hand through his hair. I felt like I was watching a commercial for shampoo. "Well, I think it's juvenile to think that Mrs. Frankweiler wasn't family. Didn't you get the feeling that they adopted her as a grandmother? Family can be people we choose. Sometimes family is who you choose to love, sometimes it is who is there for you, and sometimes it's who you learn from."

Did this guy call me juvenile? Even more ridiculous.

"And what exactly did they learn from Mrs. Frankweiler?" I asked.

Mrs. Gaarder stepped in. "I was about to pose that same question to the *class*," she said, "with a follow-up. What did the kids learn from Mrs. Frankweiler, and what did Mrs. Frankweiler learn from the *kids*?"

Cool guy nodded to Mrs. Gaarder.

"Anyone?" Mrs. Gaarder asked.

"Umm, yeah." Jack straightened up in his chair and pushed his hood down to his shoulders. "The obvious response is that Mrs. Frankweiler helped Claudia find the answer to the mystery they were looking for. She helped them find out whether the Michelangelo statue was real or not." Jack spoke confidently. *Articulate*. I hated him more.

"But I think she and Claudia had a real bond because they were so alike. They got each other. Mrs. Frankweiler knew what Claudia needed to find before she could go home."

Jack pulled one drawstring on his hood all the way down so it tightened into a little ball at the back of his neck.

"Mrs. Frankweiler liked having secrets," Jack continued, "just for the sake of having a secret. She understood that Claudia would too."

He pulled the other drawstring, loosening the tension.

"When Claudia had a secret of her own, she was ready to go back home. I think that's what she was looking for—a reason to go back home. And that couldn't really be found in the files."

Claudia was looking for answers in the wrong place. Like old school newspapers.

CHAPTER
THIRTY-FIVE

My first water park experience was more fun than expected, and my first scary movie didn't live up to the hype. I've noticed most things in life are like that: better or worse than the expectation. My first Minnesota winter, however, lived up to its reputation. The sun went down before it had a chance to go up, my big toe went numb in the time it took me to walk the trash cans to the curb, and I told Sara that seeing my breath in the cold was happiness leaving my body. I was only half joking. Twice, school was canceled because it was too cold. I'm not talking about snow days. Snow days were for wimps. Minnesotans called off school after calculating time spent getting to the bus stop before frostbite set in. We're talking potential loss of limb. See, it lived up to its reputation. Others were running outside, skiing, snowboarding, skating, sledding, snowshoeing, and building forts. I spent a lot of time indoors that winter.

In Hawaii, winter break meant baking Christmas cookies at a friend's house, where there'd be a present for Sara and me under their tree, just as there were always new clothes and cash for them at Eid. Here, we'd watched our second movie about reindeer and Christmas spirit found before Mom turned off the TV.

"That was the hospital," she said, putting her phone down. "Dad's doing better. They're even talking about trying to get him off the ventilator tomorrow." She got off the couch with a little hop and a smile. "Why don't we take a drive to see everyone's Christmas lights?" she asked.

Sara was up in a second.

I looked outside and saw snow blowing over the top of the birdhouse. Blowing snow was already my least favorite.

"I don't think so," I replied.

Mom picked up her keys from the counter. "It was more command than request. Let's go."

We passed Jack's house, the only other home that didn't have Christmas lights, and drove around oohing and aahing over the ones that did. I liked the houses done completely in white. Sara, of course, liked the ones with the big inflatable reindeer and Santa in the front. Mom's favorites were the colorful ones.

"Would you still visit me if I celebrate Christmas when I grow up?" Sara asked.

"Of course I would. But I hope you'd want to celebrate Eid as well," Mom answered.

"Totally. I would do both."

Celebrating Christmas had been an ongoing argument for years in our house, a one-sided one. I had begged and pleaded when I was younger to get a tree, hang some lights, exchange a few gifts. Neither parent budged. I had threatened, more than once, to grow up and celebrate Christmas all year round. Mom had shrugged. Dad didn't bother looking up. Yes, it would be great to get a nice pile of gifts, but Eid came twice a year instead of once, and I preferred cash to socks, so I got over it. It was Sara's turn now.

"Then what about Hanukkah and Diwali and the holidays that Buddhists and Baha'i and Sikhs and everyone else celebrate?" I asked.

"Wow, imagine all the gifts. All year around," Sara answered. That must have been too much for her to wrap her mind around, because soon after that she fell asleep. The music was on, the Christmas lights looked foggy through the snow, and Sara was snoring lightly in the backseat. The snow lightened to a flurry like a snow globe right before it settled and just before you were tempted to shake it again.

Mom was telling me the story of when she was the Cheshire Cat in her school's production of *Alice in Wonderland* years ago, and how they had Indianized their version by making Alice eat a samosa to get bigger and smaller. "Dad's school did *Alice in Wonderland* when he was in elementary school, too," I said, "but I'm guessing they did the version without the samosas."

She laughed. "Did Dad tell you about that? Was he in the play?"

"No. I've been looking through old newspapers at school."

She turned the volume down. "Hmm?"

"I was looking for stuff about Dad. And his brother."

I expected each piece of information I found about them to satisfy me, but it only made me want more. Like those snack-sized chips that were always too small, I'd get to the bottom of the bag, use my licked fingers to pick up the crumbs, and still be hungry. I found lots of things about my father: photos, his name on school teams, others talking about him in quotes describing their favorite memories. The only time I found my uncle's name was on the list of science fair contestants, not on the list of winners, only the list of contestants. I could count that on one chip-covered finger. There were never enough crumbs. *Unsatiated.*

"What were you hoping to find, Ahmed?" Mom asked as we pulled into our garage.

"I don't know really. Dad said he wished he had more stuff of his brother's. I guess I wanted to help him have some."

Mom carried Sara inside. I hadn't seen her do that in years. She set Sara down on the couch before handing me an envelope from the drawer next to the purple chair. "I don't know if this is the kind of thing you were looking for. It's Mohammed's obituary."

The folder was thin, with only a few pieces of paper at the bottom.

There was a picture of my uncle, and underneath the photo, a few words.

> *In memory of Mohammed Aziz (1974–1986).*
> *Mohammed will always be remembered for his quiet demeanor.*
> *He was always happy to let others shine.*
> *He will be missed.*

I was surprised that's all it said, as if my hours of searching meant there had to be more. I was still holding the paper when Mom came down after tucking Sara in.

"That's all it said?" I asked as I handed it back to her. I had never met my uncle or spoken to him, so why did it feel like it wasn't enough?

"Yes, honey, that's all it said." Mom stepped closer to me.

"You know, I think we would have really gotten along—my uncle and I."

"I think you're absolutely right," Mom said. She pushed some hair off my forehead.

Hours spent sneezing and coughing in the dust of the school library, and this had been in my house the whole time, right under my nose.

A handful of nonspecific, generic, could-have-been-about-anybody words.

I looked at the picture attached to the obituary. It was the same photo that hung over my locker. He was off to the side of the frame both there and here. He wasn't even in the center of his own death. I read the words again, and it made me sad. Not sad in the way deaths are supposed to, but sad that there was nothing more to say about him. Those words could have been used to describe anybody, to describe me. His whole life covered in three lines.

"Why is this so short?"

"I don't know, Ahmed," she answered. "Sometimes it's hard to find the right words."

CHAPTER
THIRTY-SIX

I woke up the next morning feeling uncomfortable inside. Something about reading my uncle's obituary. *Unsettled.* Sara and I called it the overdue-library-book feeling. One of the few things that made Dad mad was an overdue library book. Luckily it was a rare day that I had a book checked out. Sara was the bigger culprit. But one day I found this great book about artificial intelligence, and it was nine p.m. when I realized it was overdue. I couldn't sleep the whole night, twisting my sheets into a ball at the foot of my bed. That feeling didn't go away until I returned the book the next day. Since then, if either Sara or I felt restless or jittery, we called it the overdue-library-book feeling. One more reason to dislike books.

I woke up thinking about Claudia, because it was

suddenly clear what made her run away. She felt restless and jittery. And she couldn't pay the ten-cent fine, return the book, and make it go away. She hated the way people saw her as just "Straight-A Claudia," and she was sick of not feeling important. She ran away because she wanted to find a way to stand out.

Standing out had never been my thing. I was a blend-in sort of guy. But blending in wasn't working for me. I read my uncle's obituary again. Blending in hadn't worked for my uncle either.

Claudia copied the way a woman in a sari walked and moved, hoping that would help her stand out. Maybe that's what I needed.

I came down for breakfast wearing an old pair of jeans with holes at the knees, and an Aloha-print button-down shirt I had been given as a gag gift on my last birthday. My hair lightly crackled when I touched the top of my gelled faux-hawk. I put on a thick gold chain, a remnant from a Halloween costume, but took it off. It was too much.

Mom looked up, her eyes wide, but said only, "Good morning." I was going to try out being a new man today.

Sara wasn't as subtle. "What the . . ." I saw Mom lift her head ever so slightly and give Sara a look that shut her up.

We ate breakfast in silence.

With my jacket and hat on, I was protected from the cold and hopefully protected from Jack. I was already losing some of that confidence I pretended I had when I got dressed that morning. I pulled my hat low and kept both hands on the flaps. It must have been obvious I was trying to hide something, because Jack grabbed the pom-pom at the top of my hat and pulled it off, like a waiter unveiling the main course in front of you. "Whoa," he laughed, "just when I thought you couldn't look any dumber, you pull this." He laughed so hard he had to hold his stomach.

He threw the hat back at me. "Here, put it back on. Even I don't want to see that."

I caught my hat but left it off in defiance. "Actually, I think I'll leave it off, thank you very much."

"Look at that guy's hair," he yelled when his friend got on the bus. "He deserves every ounce of what's coming to him."

After hanging my jacket and hat in my locker, I felt as silly as I must have looked. Carl, ever so polite, was the first to notice. "What the heck is going on with you?" he asked.

"It's a new Ahmed, man. A new Ahmed," I replied.

"What was wrong with the old one?" he said.

"You have no idea, Carl."

A couple of times throughout the day, I tried to match my personality to my clothes. I laughed louder at jokes and said hi to people I normally wouldn't, yelling it louder than I needed to. To get my outsides to match my outsides, while nothing matched my insides.

I deflected and dodged multiple questions and strange looks. It was exhausting being that guy. It was even more exhausting pretending to be that guy.

I left lunch to get to Mrs. Gaarder's class, where I could turn it off for a while, already regretting my decision to follow in Claudia's footsteps. After all, it hadn't worked for her either.

"What's going on here, Ahmed?" she asked.

"What are you talking about?" I asked back.

She crossed her arms in front of her and waited.

"I thought I'd try something new."

She pushed her glasses to the top of her head and squinted, like she was taking a better look.

She put her glasses back on her face. "And what do you think?"

I wasn't sure what to think.

CHAPTER
THIRTY-SEVEN

My phone buzzed while I was waiting for Mom to pick me up to go to the hospital. *Running 10 minutes late. DAD IS OFF THE VENTILATOR* ☺ ☺

The overdue-library-book feeling I had been carrying around since morning finally went away. I felt like I could breathe again.

I waited by the bulletin board outside the school counselor's office. It was a magnetic whiteboard as high as the door and as wide as our TV. Flyers and drawings advertising different clubs and teams hung behind multicolored magnets. One of the papers was a countdown to the "Are you smarter than Mrs. Gaarder?" contest. Unrequested replies were scribbled underneath.

"This year, Mrs. Gaarder, you're going down."

"Almost beat her three years ago."

"Come on, guys. This is the year."

I laughed when a minute ago it wouldn't have seemed funny.

Carl stopped next to me. "You thinking about joining a club, Ahmed?"

I looked over the board. Football. Debate Team. Student Council.

"Nah. I'm not much of a joiner."

Carl moved around some of the overlapping flyers, looking for something. "Ahmed may not be a joiner, but maybe New Ahmed is," he said with a smile. "What about this one? I'm in it."

Hearing Dad was breathing on his own made me feel lighter. I pressed my faux-hawk down a little, embarrassed at the idea of Dad seeing it.

Media Club? I remember seeing Carl struggle with the microphones at the pep rally.

I had never joined a team in my life, but it seemed easier than faux-hawking my hair every morning. The gel was giving me a headache.

Come be part of our team! All you need is an interest in all things technology. If you spend hours watching YouTube videos of smartphone reviews and know how to unbox a set of headphones, we may be the right club

for you. We spend time talking about and sharing any
new technology out there. We also run the media for
Morning Report, put together the Student of the Month
video, and help with school plays and dances.
We meet every Tuesday after school in Room 21.

Like everyone at school, I watched the ten-minute Morning Report in homeroom. Three kids sat at a desk, like news reporters reading from a teleprompter. More times than not, the video went out, the audio was spotty, or someone dropped the camera. They needed help— maybe my help.

"We have a meeting after school today. You should come." Carl ripped the tear-off at the bottom of the flyer for me, and I took it.

"My mom's picking me up now, but I'll think about it."

Sara was in the backseat when Mom pulled up, waving at me with both hands.

"Excited to go see Dad?" Mom asked.

For the first time in a long while, I was. "Did you see him already?" I asked.

She looked over her shoulder before moving out of the parking lot. "Not yet. They just called to tell me it went okay. I thought we could see him together."

Sara was bouncing in the backseat. Literally.

"What's in your hand, Ahmed?" Mom asked. "Wait, are you thinking of joining a club?"

I looked at the tear-off about Media Club that Carl had given me. "I haven't decided yet."

There was no more tube in Dad's mouth, which meant that for the first time in a long while, we could see his whole face again. He opened his eyes when the nurse came to check on him, but shut them almost immediately. "He's holding strong," she said, after asking him to squeeze her hand. "That's a good sign."

Mom ran her hand over his cheek, then cupped his face in both hands.

Sara kissed him on his cheek and told him all about a new turn she was practicing in ballet. "And you'll never guess what, Dad," she said. "Ahmed's joining a club at school."

Mom hummed. I can't remember the last time Mom hummed. "You off the ventilator and Ahmed joining a club. Today's miracles keep coming." And she laughed, which made me smile.

CHAPTER
THIRTY-EIGHT

The next day, I told Carl I might join Media Club. Sara told Dad I was going to join, and now I couldn't go back. I didn't want Dad to wake up to a lie. Plus I was in no position to turn away miracles.

"Just show up after school next week," Carl said. "That's all you need to do." I liked the ease of it. "Didn't want to keep the cool hair?" I nodded *no*. I didn't want Dad to wake up to that lie either.

Ari and Jessica entered the classroom. "Wait," Jessica said, "what's happening after school?"

"Media Club," Carl answered.

"Yuck," Jessica replied.

"What day?" Ari asked. It seemed like me joining a club had become everyone's business.

"Great, that means you're free on Friday. A few of us

are going tubing after school. You should come."

"Doesn't sound like my kind of thing." Friday was the release date of the next version of my favorite video game. "Besides, I don't know how to go tubing."

Ari rolled his wheelchair backward and turned. "Man, there's nothing to know. You sit down and let gravity do the work. My dad will take us."

"Umm, let me think about it." Maybe new Ahmed was a joiner, but I didn't need to overdo it.

There were six of us waiting to be picked up by Ari's dad, but I was the only one stamping my feet and pulling my hood over my ears to stay warm. "What is it? Like three below zero?" I asked, watching my bus pull away, wishing, for once, I was on it.

They all started to laugh. "Three below zero was months ago. Tomorrow it's supposed to be thirty below zero."

This was funny to them?

Ari pointed at a squirrel. "Ha! No footprints in the snow, Kevin," he said, and they high-fived.

"And that's exciting?" I asked, watching footprint-less squirrels that were already thinner than last month.

"No footprints means the ground is more ice than snow," Carl explained. "More ice means more speed."

Great.

The tubing hill felt more like a mountain. Ari's dad gave us wristbands when he dropped us off. To help identify the bodies. A steep black conveyor belt at the side of the mountain—yes, I was going to call it a mountain— carried victims to the top. Ari's dad lifted him from his wheelchair and into the front of a two-person tube. I was hoping the tubes would be more secure, with harnesses and buckles, but they were just big rubber doughnuts. Not reassuring. We stood in front of our tubes holding them by ropes, like we were walking a dog. You know, if our dogs were rings of death. "You boys need me to come up with you or you think you've got this?" Ari's dad asked.

"We've got this, sir," Kevin said.

"Not like you had it last time, right, Kevin?" Ari's dad asked.

"Nope, we've really got it this time," Carl answered.

Ari put his hands on his forehead. "I told you, Dad, my rope slipped out of his hand last time."

The conveyor belt carried us to the top, and I lowered myself into the ring, butt hanging in the middle, waiting for instructions. The teenager in charge didn't take his eyes off his phone to see the fear on my face.

"Spin or no spin?" he asked.

"Huh?" I waited for clarification and preferably a video with detailed instructions.

"Spin or no spin?" He looked up from his phone, the annoyance in his voice mirrored in his face.

"No spin," I answered. Definitely no spin.

He gave my tube a push with his foot, with little thought. *Unceremoniously.* I grabbed the handles because my life depended on it. The first seconds were not bad, but I was building momentum, I learned. Soon I was off. Trees blurred in my peripheral vision, the cold stung my eyes making them water, my nose ran, and the tube threatened to slip out of my lane. I couldn't take a full breath with the weight of the cold against my chest. I felt my hat slip higher on my forehead. I released one hand from its death grip, pulled my hat down, and replaced my hand; the whole movement took less than a second, but it gave me the courage to look around. Carl and Ari were spinning down with their hands in the air. Carl had his eyes closed, and both had roller-coaster screams. I put one hand in the air like I had a question no one was going to slow down to answer. It felt like I was flying. I lifted the other. I closed my eyes and added my whoop to the others just as I hit a bump, sending me flying in one direction while the tube stayed on trajectory, landing in the orange nets at the bottom.

Carl was already out of his tube, rope in both hands, walking backward to pull Ari back to the conveyor belt.

"Man, I should have warned you. Always hold on at the bottom," Ari said.

I ran down and untangled my tube from the net, moving it out of the path before the next rider came crashing into me.

"So," Carl yelled, "what did you think?"

"Next time with a spin. Definitely with a spin."

In first grade our class had to wake up early one Saturday to plant flowers for Earth Day. I was the only one not excited about the waffle breakfast after. At home we eat all our meals with our hands, like over a billion other Indians, Mom liked to say. At age seven, I could stab a piece of meat with a fork, but I looked like a Neanderthal doing it. Mom made waffles shaped like sticks that I could hold with either hand to dip in the syrup. The waffles served that morning were the kind you cut with a fork and knife. You know, like everyone else in the world serves. I stared at eleven boys deftly cutting their waffles like the utensils were extensions of their hands. I told them I wasn't hungry and didn't eat a thing that morning, the smell of waffles and syrup twisting my stomach. For the first time since the move, I felt like I fit in, like I wasn't watching everyone else doing things

I couldn't or wouldn't. I wasn't hungry when everyone else was full.

We went up the belt and down the hill until the floodlights had to be turned on and Ari's dad called us in. I was having fun. In the snow. In Minnesota.

CHAPTER
THIRTY-NINE

I no longer felt like throwing up at the thought of class. Maybe that's what made Mrs. Gaarder a legend. It snuck up on you.

"I can't wait to hear what you have to say to-*day*," she said. "I especially love to hear who you liked or who you didn't. Any volunteers to present this mor-*ning*?"

A girl on my right raised her hand and got up. When Dad returned from a trip to Singapore, he brought back cake from the infamous durian fruit. The fruit is so smelly it's banned in airports and hotels, so he brought back the cake. He dared me to have a piece, just a small sliver, he said. Having eaten Indian food all my life, I thought my palate was ready for anything. Something with the word *cake* in it had to be, well, a piece of cake. One bite and I realized how wrong I was. It felt like something had curled up and died in my mouth, and drinking water to dilute the taste only intensified it. The expression on the girl's face, her hand still partially raised as she stood in front of us, reminded me of that. Total and utter regret.

"Umm. Yeah. So, there were, like, only a few characters in the book," she started. "Umm . . . yeah." My stomach flipped for her. "So maybe we might, I mean I thought we could, umm, talk about Mrs. Frankweiler, since she's like right in the title and all."

She paused with her mouth open but shut it again before words came out. Opened again, but shut as quickly. She looked like a fish, and not the graceful kind with bright yellow tails grouped around pink coral that you see on posters of Australia. She was floundering. I waited for someone to rescue the girl gasping for words. Mrs. Gaarder showed no signs of standing up from her chair, Carl had his head buried in his notebook, Ari was fiddling with the zipper on his sweatshirt. Come on, Jessica. No one budged. I raised my hand, taking a bullet for a fellow soldier.

"Mrs. Frankweiler really only showed up in the end of the book and was only there for a couple of chapters. I thought it was kind of strange that her name was in the title. Didn't you?"

"Umm . . . uh . . . yeah."

"I guess she was still important," I continued, "since the answer to the mystery came from her, after all."

It got things going, and Ari picked up where I left off. "Even though they only met her at the end, she's the narrator throughout the book."

Carl came in to help next, and Carl being Carl, he took over most of the class from there. "I know she isn't very popular, but my favorite character is Claudia," he said. "She was such a contradiction. She ran away from rules but ended up making rules for herself." The girl's shoulders relaxed, and her mouth finally stayed closed. "She made them change into PJs, wash their clothes, take baths, and even go to church on Sundays. Stricter than most parents." Carl could go on and on if we let him. "And isn't it strange that she ran away to be free but picked a place where they were locked up every night? Where's the freedom there?"

"Well, that makes sense," Jack replied. "Even though she chose to get away from her family, she must have missed them. Putting a schedule in place, making them wash their clothes, all of that was to keep things a little familiar. She wasn't ready to let all of that go."

The girl stopped fiddling with her necklace and mouthed "thank you" to me. I nodded back. No soldier left behind.

We talked the three characters to death, the moderator not speaking another word.

After school, I waited in Room 21 for my first meeting of Media Club. There was no grown-up running the show, which immediately made it the best club I had ever joined. Also the only club I had ever joined. There were five boys and four girls, and now there was me. One guy actually wore white tube socks with sandals, and, no joke, he had a pocket protector in the front pocket of his button-down shirt. The rest of them, though, looked like any other kids, not the movie version of a nerd. After all, Bill Gates, Steve Jobs, and Elon Musk had made being a nerd sort of cool. Just not in middle school.

We talked about phones and new software, games we had played, favorite headphones, and wish lists. It felt natural, and easy, and fun. It didn't feel like work, like that day of gelling my hair and wearing strange clothes did. Like Claudia feeling ready to go home when she learned the secret about the statue, you just knew when things felt right.

CHAPTER
FORTY

"Who's up for a Byoola day?" Mom asked.

Sara and I could barely hold our heads up, and it was so dark outside, the only indication it was morning was the cereal bowls in front of us.

"For real?" Sara asked, and I waited for the answer too.

"For real," Mom said. "I just got a call from the nurses at the hospital. Dad's moving out of the ICU tomorrow." Every day that week, the nurses were excited about his progress, but I was afraid to get my hopes up. "Getting out of the ICU. I think that deserves a Byoola."

Sara jumped off her seat, did a little dance, and hugged Mom so tight that she almost fell. I did the same. In my head.

A Byoola day was a Dad invention. Years ago, we watched an old movie about this high school kid who took the day off school and spent the whole day doing fun, wild things. Dad thought we should do the same, and once or twice a year when we really needed it, we'd all take the day off. Sometimes we'd do fun, wild things ourselves. And sometimes we'd sit at home and watch movies. Whatever we wanted. That was the beauty of a Byoola day. I don't remember the name of the movie, but the kid's last name was Bueller, which Sara pronounced *Byoola*. And that's how Byoola days came to be a thing.

"How do you want to spend it?" Mom asked.

Sara and I looked at each other and answered almost in unison. "With Dad."

Dad looked more like Dad. Every day we visited, there was one less line going into him and one less tube coming out. They let us bring a blanket from home, and Sara picked his favorite green one with the paisleys on it. His room was decorated with Sara's paintings taped to the window, and photos of us in frames stood on the windowsill. Cards and balloons crowded every free corner.

The nurses in the ICU walked with a quick step, quiet in their white tennis shoes, busy checking meters, turning off alarms, emptying and filling bags, all with a look of worry and seriousness about them. Today they were different. Their steps were slower, and they chatted while they worked. As if time had slowed down, as if they had more of it, as if we had more of it.

"Excited to have your dad come home soon?"

"No way," Sara said, not wanting to take for granted our good fortune for the second time that day.

"Sure. Maybe another week tops if everything goes well. We're sick of him. Take him home already." And they all laughed like it was the funniest joke in the world.

Sara told Dad every thought that crossed her mind. This time I had something to say as well. I told him about Media Club and running Morning Report, and how fast that hour flew by every week.

A lady with a gray bun and a curved back traveled from room to room with coffee and tea and a rolling case of books. I picked *Bridge to Terabithia* to kill two birds with one stone. I told her this when I borrowed the book and she suggested I not use the word *kill* in the ICU. Dad stayed awake for minutes at a time now, but Mom joked that the shock of hearing me read might be the thing to keep him awake.

He was awake long enough to know we were there, and long enough for him to smile at us. And that made it the best Byoola day yet.

CHAPTER
FORTY-ONE

Every week, Mom and Sara picked me up after Media Club. Mom had a list of restaurants that served the best Juicy Lucy burgers, and every week we'd try another one. Our plan was to vote for our favorite and take Dad when he was ready. I missed Hawaiian plate lunches, but cheese oozing out of the middle of my burger definitely made up for it. Tonight's Juicy Lucy was our third and unanimously our favorite so far.

There was a package waiting at the door when we came home, so Sara jumped out of the car before Mom had come to a complete stop. Sara got excited about every package, even when it was kitchen sponges. She begged to open it, fighting no one for the chance, making a production of it every time. I was surprised when she didn't immediately start dancing around the box.

"It's not for us."

"It's for Jack's mom. Ahmed, can you run it over there?" Mom asked.

"Can't Sara do it this once?" Dad's improvements, Media Club, a burger still in my belly—I was in too good a mood to step onto Jack's porch.

"It will just take a minute, Ahmed."

The package was heavy and there was still ice on the ground, so I slipped a couple of times. I hoped the contents were worth it. Their porch lights were on. I tried to be as quiet as possible to drop the package and run, but the front door opened before I could set it down.

"Hi!" It was Jack's mom. "Thank you so much. I've been waiting for this package all day. They said it was delivered hours ago, and I was getting anxious. Why don't you come in . . ."

"Ahmed." I filled in her blanks. I had met her enough times that she should have remembered.

"Thanks, Mrs. Hanson, but I have a lot of homework to get done." She took the package from me and set it down.

"How is school going?"

"Fine, I guess."

"Are you spending more time on schoolwork or on social media? What's that app your school has?"

"Umm, Connect. No, I'm not on there much. I use it for my homework assignments mainly." I took a step back to let her know I was ready to go.

"Really?" she asked. "Jack makes it sound like it's the most important thing in the world. He spends hours on there."

Jack stood behind her. It was strange to see him in his natural habitat, wearing pajamas too short for him. "I mean, yeah, it is super important," I said, trying to backpedal. "All the kids talk about is how many followers they have." Not true.

His mom turned to look at him, and I could see he was turning red.

"Jack has the most followers of anyone in school."

She ruffled Jack's hair in a show of affection, but her words didn't strike me as being affectionate. "Jack's always been one to try to get everyone's attention. Wouldn't be the first time he's stretched the truth a bit."

I really wanted to get off that porch and back to my house. "No, I swear, Mrs. Hanson, he does. They were even planning on making him Student of the Month because of it."

"Thanks for delivering the package . . ."

"Ahmed," I said. And I got out of there as quickly as I could.

CHAPTER
FORTY-TWO

My alarm didn't ring, but I didn't need to look at my clock to know I was late. The sun was partially out, and I could see Jack kicking a can at the bus stop already. I grabbed a T-shirt from the floor, and with one leg still in my pajama pants I ran-hopped to the bathroom. Sara had spent the evening painting in my room when Mom went back to the hospital, and my backpack knocked over the yogurt container she used to clean her brushes. Mud-colored water spilled all over her painting of the beach, turning her sunny day into a cloudy one in one klutzy moment. The water spilled over the edge of the table, my backpack and pants collateral damage. I pulled out my uncle's copy of *Bridge to Terabithia*, the corner soaking wet. "Saaaarrrraaaa!" I screamed, but she was long gone. The bus honked its horn, so I rescued my laptop from the bag, pulled on my pants, and ran for it. I missed the comfort of having his book.

By the time I got to school, the back of my pants was crusty and stiff from the paint water. I didn't notice, at first, the small crowd gathering around my locker. It was a crowd of four, but it felt like more. The principal, the custodian, and two police officers. From that moment until the end of that very long day, things moved in slow motion.

Sara forced me to watch a mermaid movie once. It was totally forgettable, except for one scene. The mermaid was underwater with the reflection of the sun above her and little bubbles popping out of her mouth, her long hair lifted all around her face like a mane, and when she turned, her hair responded slowly, following her movements slower than the rest of her. That's how it was: like I was present but slow to catch up.

I saw the principal's tie with a snowman, and noticed the snowman had a big smile. But it took me longer to notice that no one else was smiling. I saw the custodian had opened a locker for them. But it took me longer to notice the locker was mine. I saw two police officers flanking Principal Roberts, hands held behind their back in a show of force. But it took me longer to understand it was me they were waiting for. I waited for someone to yell "April Fools" so everyone could let out the laugh that must have been hiding behind those serious expressions. But it was March.

One policeman was short, his bright red face bathed in sweat. He kept tugging his collar. The other officer was a woman, tall and skinny with blond hair in a ponytail, hat tucked under her right arm. Her face looked naked and pinched, like she had worn glasses all her life and was adjusting without them. The four of them stood in a tight circle until Mr. Roberts broke away toward me.

"Ahmed, we need to have a word with you."

"Umm. Sure," I answered. "What's going on?"

"Let's discuss this in my office." The sweaty officer reached his hand out for my laptop and I gave it to him like I had no choice. He and the custodian went one way, while the three of us went the other, walking shoulder to shoulder, filling half the hall. *Abreast.*

We walked to the principal's office and into a small conference room, no one telling the other where we were headed. The idea that police officers and the principal had spent the morning discussing where they would take me felt unreal.

The conference room had a long table with eight chairs around it. A pitcher of water was in the middle, with upside-down paper cups wrapped in cellophane next to it. There was a pink poster on the wall with a unicorn flying in the middle. *Let your imagination help you fly* was written in glitter across the bottom. The principal sat at the head of the table and gestured for me to sit in the middle. I did not. The police officer sat on the long side of the table directly below the unicorn poster. It looked like glitter was coming out of the unicorn's butt and landing on her head.

"I'm Officer Jen," said ponytail.

She pointed to the seat across from her, but I remained standing. I should sit down, I thought to myself. I couldn't get my body to obey.

"Is my dad okay?" I asked.

"Why wouldn't he be?" asked Officer Jen. She answered a question with a question. Mom would have given her that look. "Is your dad part of this?"

What were they talking about?

"Why don't you have a seat, Ahmed?" Mr. Roberts asked.

I couldn't get myself to move.

"This will be a lot easier if you cooperate, Ahmed," Officer Jen said.

Cooperate with what? I wondered. But not out loud.

"How come you don't have a backpack today? Unusual to come to school without your backpack, isn't it?"

I'm pretty sure that wasn't the unusual part of the day. If I could get my body to move, I would turn around so they could see the stain on the back of my pants where the dirty paint water had dried. That would clear up the whole thing, wouldn't it?

"Were you expecting us at your locker this morning?"

Sure, like a fly expects a spiderweb.

Sweaty face walked in. I wanted to tell him to wipe his face. "Ahmed, I'm Officer Max." He looked at Officer Jen. "Trash cans are all clear."

He took a seat next to Officer Jen. Everyone knew their cues in this play except me. "Ahmed, if you'd answer our questions to the best of your ability, things should go smoothly. You're not in any trouble. We just have some questions to ask you."

It sure felt like I was in trouble.

"We're here today, Ahmed, because of a photograph." She put her hat on the table. "We were alerted, this morning, to a very disturbing photo of you, a photo suggesting that you may be planning an attack." She picked up her hat again and put it on her lap.

An attack? With ninjas and nunchucks?

Officer Jen answered my thoughts. "An attack on this school."

I continued to stand there perfectly still, not giving

212

away the hurricane inside, apparently incriminating myself by doing so. I opened my mouth to speak, but my tongue was dry, like kindling Mom asked us to find on that family camping trip she forced us on. If I moved my tongue, I could breathe fire.

"I really wish you'd cooperate, Ahmed." The way she stressed the *h* in my name sounded like a *kh*, and it hurt my ears. "We just need you to answer our questions, and we can get on with things." She waited for me to say something. "Akhmed, your silence isn't reassuring."

I hadn't realized I was supposed to be reassuring them.

"These are very serious allegations. I hope you understand that. Telling us what you know would be best for you," she said, "and your father."

I hadn't moved from my spot. Mom had an uncle who, at age nine, on his way back from a cricket game, came across a cobra in the middle of the road. The story goes that before the cobra had a chance to raise its head, he whacked it with his cricket bat, killing it with one stroke. He was nicknamed Killer that day, and the story was retold at every family gathering. When I finally met Killer, I asked him about it, but he said he couldn't remember a thing, that it was pure adrenaline. It was flight or fight, and he had fought. I always wondered how I would have responded. Would I fight or would I fly? Turns out I'd do neither.

The principal finally had something to say. "Perhaps we can try giving his parents a call again." He pulled a card from his jacket pocket and dialed. I could hear Mom's voice asking him to leave a message. "Hello, Mrs. Aziz. This is Principal Roberts calling from Ahmed's school again. It's extremely important you call us back as soon as you get this message."

"Very important," he added, in case she didn't understand.

Officer Jen stood up and walked around the table to stand next to me. I could smell her gum. Spearmint.

"We have to do this by the book, Ahmed. I'm so sorry, honey," she said, her tone apologetic. "You have the right to remain silent. Anything you say can and will be used against you in a court of law."

We were quite the group in the conference room. One cop sweaty, one pinch-faced, an unhelpful principal, and a silent boy, none of us ready to make the next move, all of us uncomfortable.

Mr. Roberts got up to open the door, letting in laughter from the office. The sound seemed so out of place, I turned toward it. Mrs. Gaarder was there, and her laughter stopped mid-breath and her smile slipped off her face.

She walked into the conference room to stand next to me, facing the officers. She had her hands on her hips. Like Wonder Woman.

"Exactly what is going on here?" she asked. I hardly recognized her voice. It was loud and strong, and there was no up curve at the end.

"Ma'am, this has nothing to do with you."

"I couldn't disagree more. This is one of my students, so it has everything to do with me. I will ask you again, Officer. What is going on here?"

Officer Max found that moment to wipe his forehead, finally. "We are in the middle of an investigation, ma'am," he said. "We are not yet ready to share information." He walked around the table to stand in front of Mrs. Gaarder. She looked him up and down, and he pulled on his collar again. Officer Jen tucked a piece of hair behind her ear. Mr. Roberts picked up the papers in front of him.

"If you're thinking about interrogating one of my students, you most certainly better be ready."

Officer Max squared his shoulders back to stand taller. "The safety of this school is our only concern at this time."

"I understand that. I do. But you had better make sure what you're doing here is legal. Make sure all your *t*'s are crossed and *i*'s are dotted, sir." Like a homework assign-ment. "Why is his mother not here?"

"We tried, Janet. I've left her three messages," Princi-pal Roberts replied.

"You left her a message?" She was practically scream-ing. "You left her a message? Let me get this straight. One of our students, a twelve-year-old, is being questioned by police officers, and you left his mom a message? Does that sound remotely sufficient, Mr. Roberts?"

I thought he might cry.

"Umm. I feel badly about this—" Officer Jen started.

"Bad. You feel bad, Officer," she corrected her.

"We don't want to do this. I have kids, too, you know. But you must understand how important it is to keep the students in this school safe. I really wish he'd answer our questions, but he hasn't said a word." She shifted her weight to one leg and then the other.

"Why don't we try again, Officer . . ."

"Jen. Officer Jennifer Edmonton."

Mrs. Gaarder dialed a number and gestured for me to sit down. I finally did. Turns out the five feet that made up Mrs. Gaarder was more powerful than everyone in that room.

"I got voice mail, Ahmed. Let me try the hospital." But there was no answer. "Why don't we all sit down? I'm sure his mom will call back." Mrs. Gaarder put her hand on my shoulder.

Through the open door, the secretary's chair let out a high, shrill squeak as she sat down. Everyone turned to look at her. "I need to get that fixed," she mumbled. Everyone was having a bad day.

"Based on the charges we have against him, we have the right to question him without his parents' consent," Officer Max said.

"Having the right doesn't make it right, Officer."

Mrs. Gaarder turned to the secretary. "Would you mind finding someone to take over my class while I stay here?" She closed the door and returned to sit next to me.

Somewhere in the hall I heard a kid yelling. A kid gloriously in that hall instead of this hell.

"Ma'am," Officer Max said and sighed, "we don't want to do this any more than you would. But it's our job, and we have to take this seriously."

Mrs. Gaarder placed her hands, fingers entwined, on the table, ready for business.

"I understand that. But I know Ahmed, and I've known his family for years. This has to be a misunderstanding. I'm sure we can get to the bottom of this. Together."

I heard someone use the word *surreal* once and wondered what it meant. Not the definition of it, but what it actually meant. I'll tell you. Surreal is feeling glad your teacher with the reputation of being legendary is the one sitting next to you. So cops can question you. After you've been read your Miranda rights. It's not a great feeling. I don't recommend it.

"Ahmed, it's going to be okay." Mrs. Gaarder put her hand on my arm. "I know you haven't done anything wrong, but we need to figure this out. Why don't you tell us what this is about now?" I thought she was talking to me, but she turned her body to face the officers across the table.

Officer Jen took the lead. "We received an anonymous tip this morning. We were told to look at your school website, where we found a photo of Ahmed." She straightened the box of tissues in front of her. "A photo we had to investigate immediately." She moved her hands to her lap. "Because it showed Ahmed making a threat against the school."

Mrs. Gaarder looked at me. If it took her by surprise, she didn't let me see it. "Any idea what they're talking about, Ahmed? Something you could have meant as a joke?"

I couldn't think of anything.

"Could we see the photo, Officer?" Mrs. Gaarder asked.

Mr. Roberts handed the officer a laptop. The computer whirred while we sat patiently and quietly, like we were waiting for a PowerPoint presentation about mitosis or algebraic proofs. She turned the laptop to face us, and I saw myself. Or a version of myself. They had zoomed in on my profile photo from school. Yes, it was definitely me, but I had a gun in my hand, and a bandanna tied around my forehead. *I expect it to be a loud bang, not a quiet soaking in* was written in red letters across my face.

I had no idea what that meant.

Our family once took photos wearing costumes from the 1920s. The photo was made to look old and yellowed. I could never make the connection between our regular family and the 1920s version of our family, which is how it felt when I looked at that photo of me.

Mrs. Gaarder didn't even blink. "Ahmed, can you explain this?"

"I didn't put that photo up, Mrs. Gaarder. That's not even me. I mean, it's me, but I've never held a gun or worn a bandanna." As if both of these held equal gravity.

"Of course I know that isn't really you, Ahmed. But do you have any idea how this was posted?"

I think I did.

"We couldn't find the source of the quote. What it was referencing . . . ," Officer Jen said.

"I know exactly what this is referencing, Officer. It's a line from the book I'm teaching in class right now, *From the Mixed-Up Files of Mrs. Basil E. Frankweiler.*"

Officer Jen signaled to Officer Max, and he scribbled something in his notebook.

"And, umm, is Ahmed, by any chance, in the class in which you teach this?"

"Yes, he is, along with thirty other kids this year."

If you took away the gun and ignored the bandanna and removed the words across my face, there was something very familiar about my goofy smile. It was the same smile plastered across the school a few months ago of me as a ballerina. It had to be Jack. "This looks Photoshopped," I suggested. *Poorly Photoshopped*, I wanted to add. I could see wavy lines in the background where he had doctored the photo. The word *doctored* made me think of Dad. I wished he was standing next to me.

"Mrs. Gaarder, it's so obvious these photos were Photoshopped. Don't they have people at the police department to prove things like this?"

The laptop screen turned black before a screensaver of a mountain range brightened it, Mrs. Gaarder's face glowing in the reflection.

"We have considered that, and we've sent it to the internet fraud department. They must be reviewing it now." Officer Max picked up the laptop as the screensaver changed to a sunset. "I'll give them a call and see what they've come up with."

Mrs. Gaarder let go of my wrist, leaving imprints of her fingers, but they faded quickly.

"Who would do this to you, Ahmed?"

"I don't know, Mrs. Gaarder." But of course I knew. I was too relieved to feel angry. I remember what Carl said about making up stories to explain Jack's behavior. *Justification*. Sometimes there's none.

Officer Max returned minutes later, laptop still in hand. "You were right, Ahmed. The photo was definitely Photoshopped." For the first time that day, he wasn't beet red. "They will need some time to trace the source of the photo."

"I hope you understand why we had to take this so seriously," Officer Jen added.

Mrs. Gaarder tore off the plastic covering the cups and poured water into them before handing one to me. I think I understood, but not really. Neither of us answered her.

Principal Roberts and both the officers gathered their things to leave the conference room. "Well, I guess you're free to go." That was it? Mrs. Gaarder and I stayed seated, and I could hear her swallow as she took long sips of water.

"Wow. I'm not sure what just happened, but I'm glad

it's over. How're you doing, Ahmed?"

In a good story, I'd say something funny and the whole thing would be behind us. In a great story, Mom would run in, give me a hug, and take me home to sit around the fire while we laughed at this unbelievable mix-up. Neither was my story.

"Purple Rain" played from Mrs. Gaarder's phone, breaking the morning's slow motion, bringing me up to speed. Her ringtone reminded me of Dad. She answered Mom's call, switching to speaker phone as she explained all those voice mails. I hadn't heard that tone in Mom's voice since the day Dad went missing. Mrs. Gaarder's summary of the day's events took away from the drama of the story. "One of the kids Photoshopped Ahmed holding a gun." (You forgot the bandanna.) "But they were able to see the photo was Photoshopped." (Only after I suggested it.) "So the police came to investigate, but it was dismissed." (After a cop read me my Miranda rights.)

"Can you take me off speaker now, Janet?" And then there was silence on Mrs. Gaarder's end followed by "okays" and "umms" and "uh-huhs," but nothing I could decipher.

"What's going on, Mrs. Gaarder?"

"You'll see. I think both of us have had enough school for one day."

CHAPTER
FORTY-THREE

We found Mrs. Gaarder's blue hatchback in the parking lot. A mixture of snow, slush, and salt covered the back window: winter dirt. Someone had written *Wash me, please* in big letters. I wonder if Mrs. Gaarder had added the comma and the please.

I looked out the window at big square store after big square store, all the rooftops covered in snow, making it hard to tell where one ended and the next one began. Gray skies, not a person in sight, and dirty snow on the side of the road. It looked like the end of the world. *Postapocalyptic.* Which suited my mood perfectly.

"Do you want to talk?"

"Not really."

I replayed everything that happened to me that day, like a movie I wasn't part of. The part of Ahmed Aziz will be played by random brown boy.

"Do you want music?"

I didn't answer.

I looked at the tiny hole in my tennis shoe. If I lifted my toe, I could see the white of my sock, bright against the multiple colors of my shoe.

"We have to pick Sara up on the way home," Mrs. Gaarder said. "Your mom has a surprise for you."

I don't think my body could take any more surprises. I waited in the car while she went in to get Sara.

"Ahmed, Mrs. Gaarder says Mom has a surprise for us. Do you think she's getting me a pony?" Sara threw her backpack on the backseat before climbing in.

"I don't think so, Sara."

"Well, I think that's what it is," she continued, unfazed. The entire car ride back, all we heard about was the pony. *There's no pony!* I wanted to scream at her. Stories that we are in will never have ponies, I wanted her to know.

"Mrs. Gaarder, the surprise is a pony, right? Pleeeease tell me."

"A surprise, by definition, Sara, means I don't tell you."

The garage door was open, and Mom's car was already there.

All I wanted was to go to my room, curl into a ball, and go to sleep. My body ached, and I felt worn-out, like I had completed the longest race of my life. I was in no mood for a surprise.

Mom opened the door, her eyes filled with tears, but she pulled me into the kitchen and flipped the switch on. My eyes adjusted. In the far corner, standing in front of the purple chair, he seemed taller and was definitely thinner, but it was him.

Sara ran to him. "Dad!" she screamed.

I ran to him, too, like I was three years old, and the four of us leaned into each other, crying and laughing. I was tall enough that my cheek touched his. He smelled different, but he felt the same. I don't know how long we stood like that, but when Mom suggested we let him sit down, Mrs. Gaarder had slipped away.

CHAPTER
FORTY-FOUR

I wrapped both hands around the cup, letting the warmth creep from my hands to the rest of my body. "Coffee?" I asked her, surprised.

Dad was upstairs. It was hard to believe, and Sara kept checking to make sure it was true. I teased her about it, and when she caught me in the hallway in the middle of the night doing the same, I pretended I was going to the bathroom.

"If you're old enough to make it through yesterday, you're old enough for a cup of coffee."

The first sip was sweet and all foam.

"I'm so sorry, Ahmed, that we weren't there for you yesterday. I can't even imagine what it was like."

I wiped the foam off my upper lip. "It's okay, Mom. Mrs. Gaarder stepped in for you guys."

"And I will never be able to thank Janet enough." She used her thumb to wipe away some of the foam I missed.

"Take me through the whole day, Ahmed. Don't leave out a single detail."

I took her through my whole day. I couldn't believe that it was only yesterday; it felt so long ago. I started with the spilled dirty paint water and finished with hugging Dad in front of the purple chair, saying Jack's name out loud for the first time.

Mom didn't interrupt, although more than once I could see she wanted to. When I was done, she was crying, but for some reason I was not. She held both my hands in hers, digging her nails into my palms. "And you're sure it's Jack?"

I nodded. "He had that photo of me."

"Then we have to do something, Ahmed. I have to talk to his mom and the police, and—"

Yesterday I would have said both, but things looked different today. "Mom, I think I can take care of this on my own."

"I don't think you understand what a big deal this is, Ahmed. What a big deal it could have been. I don't want you to think it's okay that this happened."

She relaxed her grip but didn't let go.

"I know, Mom, but I want to take care of it my way."

"I don't know about that, Ahmed," she said.

There was an ongoing battle between Mom's wish to feed the birds and the squirrels' wish to feed themselves. She had moved the feeder three times, away from squirrels that climbed the handle of the patio door and lunged at the feeder. Today a bright red bird sorted through the nuts with its beak.

"Let me try, Mom. If you fix it, it will always be my mom coming to save me. And then he will never leave me alone. Give me a chance."

CHAPTER
FORTY-FIVE

Pizza and chocolate milk in hand, I looked for a spot at our usual table, but there was nothing usual about it that day. It was mobbed, leaving empty tables all around. We are a welcoming group, always scooting over for anyone looking for a place to sit, but this was ridiculous. I heard Carl's muffled voice from inside the crowd. He stood on the bench, above everyone's heads, and waved me over. He had a spot saved for me, enough room for half my butt and half my tray. "Carl, what the heck is going on? Why don't we move?" I liked having a regular table, but it seemed liked the obvious solution.

If I didn't have school on a Friday when Dad was going to the mosque, he made me go with him. I wasn't a fan. I found the azaan comforting, and the stories the imam told before prayer reminding us to be good and do good were nice, and I liked the way we made straight lines with our body, shoulder to shoulder as we bent down for prayer. What I hated about Friday prayers was the mad rush at the end to find our shoes that had been left at the mosque entrance. In everyone's hurry to get on with their day, there was pushing and shoving, and one time my left shoe was lost and I had to hop back to the car. The crowd at our lunch table gave me flashbacks to that.

A girl with a red ribbon in her hair squeezed herself between Carl and me, knocking my tray to the floor.

"I'll get another tray. No big deal. Honestly," I said when she didn't stop apologizing. I got up to restock my lunch tray, but the table let out a collective groan. That is when I realized it was me they were waiting for.

"Man, take my lunch," someone begged. "I even have a cookie. We want to hear what happened before lunch is over."

Another ring of people formed around us. "He's telling his story," someone yelled. Like bugs around our porch light, more kids showed up. Even if I wanted to get another tray, I wouldn't make it out.

"Geez, give him some room," Carl said, and shoved half his turkey sandwich into my hand.

"I heard you were handcuffed."

I took a bite of sandwich. "Not true," I said. They looked

disappointed. "But I was read my Miranda rights."

"Huh?" asked the girl with the ribbon. Someone handed me a fresh chocolate milk, and I moved it away from the edge of the table.

"You know. Like in the movies—you have the right to remain silent . . ."

I felt the crowd lean in.

"I heard you peed your pants."

This was getting away from me. "Absolutely, one hundred percent not true. Ask the principal. Ask Mrs. Gaarder. Not true."

A cookie on a napkin was being passed down and landed on the table in front of me. An offering for the god.

Carl tried to bring it back for me. "I heard you didn't rat out the guy who set you up. Even when two cops asked you to."

"Who did it?" someone yelled. The crowd pressed into me.

"Yeah, who was it?" someone else yelled.

"I ain't no snitch," I said, trying out a double negative like a tough guy. It didn't feel right.

I heard a few "wows," but lunch was over and the ring of people dissolved, patting my back and rubbing the top of my head as they did. Like the Buddha's belly at the botanical garden.

People I had never met walked me to Mrs. Gaarder's class, letting go of me only when I opened her door, where another group waited for me until I sat down. Like it was a relay and I was the baton. Everyone in class crowded around. Well, almost everyone. They didn't notice when Mrs. Gaarder came in and tried to "ahem" them back to their seats.

"Okay, everyone, settle down," she said, forcing them to their chairs. *Reluctantly.*

"Ahmed, if you'd like, you can take some time to tell your story today."

I didn't have anything prepared.

"Nah, I'm good," I replied.

"Are you sure? You could straighten the story out. In the version I heard, you single-handedly pinned down two cops and rappelled out the window to your *freedom*," she said, winking at me.

I remembered the truth: frozen in one spot, unable to speak, let alone rappel out a window. "I like that version better anyway."

Everyone laughed. Well, almost everyone.

"Since it's the last day before spring break, I'll let you spend time working on the essays for *Mixed-Up Files*. If you use your time wisely, you won't have to do any work over the break," Mrs. Gaarder said.

She referred to a paper in her hand and moved the toddler heads along. All of us strained our necks to see. We were still in second place. Not bad.

The class was quiet, all of us working individually instead of together for a change.

Jack packed his stuff to go, and I heard him telling Mrs. Gaarder he wasn't feeling well. All this attention on me must be making him feel uncomfortable, like the outsider.

I didn't mind.

BOOK
THREE

CHAPTER
FORTY-SIX

Dad was home, and besides his revolving door of appointments to the physical therapists and doctors, he was really home. I would never have to check the bathroom for his toothbrush every morning, answering whether he was home or at the hospital without having to ask the question. We didn't have to count each moment we had together as lucky and finish plans we made by saying, "Well, it all depends." The house felt different.

I took out the copy of *Bridge to Terabithia* I had been carrying from the first day of school. From the moment I saw my last name in the first page of that book, I had kept it close. I kept it in my backpack, carried it around the house, and slept with it under my pillow. I picked it up again. It was still falling apart at the seams, but having Dad at home meant I was finally ready. I was ready to read it, and I was ready to share it.

Book in hand, I wandered through the house looking for them. Dad was sleeping, and Mom was praying. It seemed to be a trend lately. The house was quiet except for the sound of Mom's whisperings and her knees clicking as she moved to kneel on the floor, pressing her forehead to the ground. I lay on the bed next to Dad, like I did when I was a kid. There was something nice about watching the rise and fall of each breath, and I put my hand on his chest.

I opened the book carefully. A few paragraphs in, I wasn't loving it. Reading the beginning out loud to my father in a hospital room had given it a sense of purpose. *Gravitas.* Reading it alone—it felt weak. Who practiced running all summer just so they could be first in a race at recess? Maybe that was important in the seventies, but kids didn't care about that anymore.

Dad stretched awake next to me and rolled to face me.

"What's going on, Ahmed? How're you doing?" He yawned and rubbed his eyes.

"Pretty good." And I have to admit, I was.

He sat up, and I moved over to allow him to swing his legs over and find his slippers. He pulled my head toward him and put his lips on my head. Dad wasn't a kisser; he was an inhaler. He inhaled me long and hard.

"Dad," I complained.

"Fine, fine, but I never thought I'd get to be here and smell these smells again."

I pulled the missing slipper from under the bed and laid it out for him. "Eau de teenage boy?"

He laughed. It was nice to be able to make him laugh again. He held a pillow against his belly, like the therapist had taught him, to help protect his sutures. "Don't make me laugh, Ahmed. I'm not sure I'm ready for that yet."

Mom finished praying and whispered Assalamu Alaikum to her right and then her left, to the two angels she had told us were on our shoulders, the angel on the right shoulder writing down every good thing we do, the angel on the left shoulder writing down every bad thing. I spent months when I was six trying to flick those angels off. They terrified me. Parents have no idea what stories to tell and what stories to keep to themselves.

The three of us walked downstairs together where Sara was setting up the carrom board. She'd been begging for a rematch ever since I beat her a few weeks ago.

Dad settled into the chair next to her, and I brought him the book. "I want to show you something, Dad."

I laid it in his lap. "You're reading this, Ahmed?"

"Yeah, I know I'm too old for it, but Mrs. Gaarder has this project and . . ."

"This was my brother's favorite book," Dad said. "It's the only book I ever remember him reading." He stroked the cover gently, like it was me or Sara. "Once they diagnosed his liver disease, he became obsessed with death." He turned the book over to look at the back. "Like he knew." He ran his thumb over the binding. "He carried it around for months."

"That's what I wanted to show you, Dad. I was waiting for you come home."

I opened the front page of the book and turned it to face Dad. He traced the name with his finger, like I had. First, he smiled. "I can't believe it," he said. "After all these years." And then he started to cry. In all my years, through everything we'd been through, through every memory of his brother he shared, through the time his parents passed away, through every hospitalization, I had never seen Dad cry like that. I didn't know what to do. I put my hand on his back, and he pulled me in. He cried like a baby. Big, heaving sobs.

"Your sutures, Dad," I reminded him, but he couldn't stop. Sara looked at Mom, bewildered. Mom looked at me, eyes wide open. Dad caught his breath and held me back by my shoulders before turning the book to chapter one. "He wrote little notes along the edges. I remember making him erase them before he returned it." We checked the first few pages, and there, along the margins of the page, in markings so light they were barely visible, were my uncle's notes. I read them out loud, going back to read the parts of the book he was talking about. Mom joined us at the table.

My uncle had the same sarcastic humor as me. We were rolling our eyes and raising our eyebrows together.

Dad interrupted my reading. "You and your uncle," he said, "two peas in a pod."

Some of the comments made us laugh, and some made me sad. He had underlined things once when they were interesting, twice when they were important, but only one sentence was underlined three times. *Thrice.* "Mrs. Meyers had helped him already by understanding that he would never forget Leslie." In his story, he was the Leslie. He was the one who died. He was the one worried about being forgotten.

By the last page it was dark outside, all of us caught in the glow of the light over our table, the rest of the house in darkness. There was one final note on the last page, not erased, written down the margin from top to bottom. Each word a little darker, each word a little bigger, each letter leaving an indentation from pencil pressed hard against paper. "Courage takes many forms," I read out loud. We all sat quietly, allowing the strangeness of reading a book with an uncle that died years ago to seep in.

As always, Sara broke the silence. "What the heck is that supposed to mean?" Mom shot her a look.

"Sorry, Mom," she said, "but what does that mean? Courage means you're brave, right? How can that have many forms?"

"What it means, Sara," I explained, "is that there are different types of courage. It took courage to go across the creek when it was raining so hard. It took courage to get revenge on their bully. It took courage for Jess to move on after his friend died." Mom turned on lights and opened the fridge to start dinner.

"Scary stuff will happen to everyone, but how you take what you're feeling and make something good out of it is what matters."

Mom and Dad both stopped what they were doing to look at me.

I leaned toward Sara with my hands in an O, pretending to strangle her. "Otherwise the scary stuff will get you."

My parents went back to what they were doing, reassured that I wasn't actually using my brain, analyzing things, and I was the same Ahmed they knew.

But that's when I got it. That's the moment it all came together for me. That would be our point of discussion in class. That could be what helped win that trophy. But also, so much more.

CHAPTER
FORTY-SEVEN

Bright grass replaced dirty snow, and trees bare and hopeless a month ago showed tiny buds.

I hadn't seen Jack all of winter break, and I didn't miss him. Standing at the bus stop, I was surprised by how ordinary he looked. Ten days ago, this guy ruled my life. Technically, I could rule his now. If I wanted to. But I had decided to take care of it myself. It felt much better to be the one in control instead of the one being controlled. Maybe that's what made him look so ordinary. He couldn't look me in the eye.

"You have anything you want to say to me, Jack?"

"Umm. No."

"You sure?"

"Umm. Yeah."

Umm, idiot.

I didn't have a plan yet, but I had learned in Mrs. Gaarder's class that being prepared and doing the research made all the difference. I started by paying attention to Jack, listening when he spoke, watching what he did, taking note of how he acted. I'm sure there's a single perfect word to describe the insanity of avoiding someone at all costs and then following them, but I couldn't think of a polite one.

I noticed a few things right away.

First of all, he had other victims. That's right: I wasn't the only one he tormented. There were a handful of us I called the Chosen Few. I was so busy dealing with how he treated me that I never realized there were others. We could have formed a club. I couldn't see myself staying after school on Tuesdays for that one.

Second, Jack was high-strung. He was always moving or fidgeting. The only time he relaxed was when he listened to music. With headphones on, the lines and furrows on his forehead disappeared, and he looked softer. I don't think I would have been able to pick out that version of Jack in a police lineup.

Third, he truly was a jerk. I saw him kick a dead bird on the sidewalk.

Following him without getting noticed was hard work, but eventually my hard work paid off.

Jack's crony: "Wicked headphones, Jack."

Jack: "I know. My mom got them for me when she went to Tokyo last week. They don't even sell them in the US yet. They're Noguchi originals."

Crony: "So what are all those buttons for, anyway?"

Jack: "I have no idea. The manual is in Japanese."

Of course I had heard of Noguchis. We had spent a whole hour at Media Club talking about them. None of us had seen a pair. We read the specs, watched videos about them, and drooled. I knew a lot more about them than Jack did. I knew the sound quality was excellent even when used with Bluetooth. I knew they were designed by the head of some fancy fashion brand in Paris. I knew they were water resistant. I also knew the buttons on the right side were the transmit button. Pressing those converted the headphones into a transmitter, allowing any speaker or screen nearby to play what you were listening to. You could transmit the music from your phone, a video you were watching, or a phone call you were on. The guy who invented them was a genius, but the guy who learned how to use them to take down his bully was a genius as well. That would be me.

I watched Jack walk away, headphones on, studying something on his phone. I zoomed in on my phone to see him better. He looked at his screen, did a strange move with his body, and looked back at his screen. Then he'd try it again. I didn't have to see what he was watching to know what he was doing. I had seen Sara do it a million times. He was trying to learn a dance. I hit record on my phone.

That was when my plan started to take shape.

CHAPTER
FORTY-EIGHT

We were starting our discussions on the third and final book. Mom politely declined taking Jack to school in the mornings. No more lectures about helping your neighbor either. Jack was the first one in the gym, and I saw him through the door, snapping his fingers and practicing spins. I added video footage to my growing collection.

I waited for the others before going in.

"I was surprised by how much I liked reading *Bridge to Terabithia* this time," Ari said. "I remember hating it before, because it was so sad. It's still sad, but there was so much more to it."

"Even though it's my first time reading it—"

Jessica interrupted me. "Wait. You've never read this book before? How's that even possible? Don't people read books in Hawaii?"

I put my pencil down. "Jessica, it'd be great if you'd let me, or anyone, finish a thought." I paused, waiting for her usual sarcastic comment.

"Fine," she replied.

She put both her elbows on the table, rested her chin in her hands, fluttered her eyes at me in an "I'm waiting" sort of way.

"What I was going to say is that I really enjoyed the book. I think we should talk about the different ways courage came up in the book. Like how Jess forced himself to be courageous, and then he found that he was." Fake it till you make it.

Jessica put her index finger up like she was telling me to wait a minute, then dramatically lifted the finger higher and flew it to her mouth like an airplane, pretending to gag on it.

"What I think our lovely friend Jessica is trying to say," Ari said, "is that maybe we should go a little deeper into the book. How about we talk about the importance of family in the book." He turned through his notes. "We've covered family in the other books, so we could do a compare-and-contrast sort of thing. I don't think family is one of the first themes that pops out, but I think it's a good one for discussion."

I looked at the clock: school was about to start.

"We can talk about how each kid was similar to their family members. Like Leslie was kind of free-spirited like her parents. And Janice was a bully, and it sounds like her dad was one too."

"Is your monologue done, Ari? I don't want to be accused of interrupting another incredible brain wave you guys are having," Jessica said.

"Well, what do you have in mind, Jessica?" I asked.

"Truth is, I don't know, but I feel we need something better and deeper to finish off the year. You haven't had much to say today, Jack. Thoughts?"

He put his pencil down. "Umm. Yeah, that's fine. Whatever."

Generally I didn't think about art much. Except the one time Mom showed me pixel art. The techie in me liked the name. I like how up close it didn't make sense, but you step far enough away and the picture comes into focus. Sometimes when you get too close to something, you can't see it clearly anymore. Chasing Jack around school and our neighborhood with my camera, I couldn't tell if he was quieter and being nicer. Or whether I had lost all perspective.

CHAPTER
FORTY-NINE

On the classroom maze, all the laminated heads were in front of the third book. Three books ago seemed like a lifetime. Our head was now an inch in front of the others. An inch seemed like a mile.

"I've enjoyed your discussions from the last two books," Mrs. Gaarder said. "Especially how you discovered things in each book that were important to you."

She picked up the trophy and polished it with the corner of her shirt. "I'm not saying any of your discoveries have been trophy worthy, or . . . what's that word you kids use . . . *baller*."

We groaned in unison. Grown-ups speaking teen was always painful.

She crossed the room and looked out the window long enough that she seemed surprised we were still there.

"That's exactly what is interesting about reading a *book*. No matter how different the characters are from us, we can find something in common with *them*. It's the author's job to offer that to you, and it's your job to find it."

She was very chatty today. She took a shawl that was hanging on her chair and wrapped herself in it with one sweep of her arm before sitting behind her desk. I thought that meant she was ready to hand the class over, but she wasn't.

"What do you, as students in a suburb of Minnesota, have in common with kids in a juvenile detention camp or kids who have run away from home?" she continued. "If you thought there was nothing, you'd be wrong, and if you don't get that from reading a book, you're losing out."

I wasn't losing out.

"It's also what makes reading a book at different stages and ages in your life a different experience. When you read *Bridge to Terabithia* in third grade, it's heartbreaking to think of your best friend dying. When you read it now, there's a lot more for you to think about. The story hasn't changed, the characters haven't changed. What's changed is you."

She looked at me.

"I believe all four teams have had a chance to moderate by now, right? I'll take any volunteers for today."

Yes, I had changed, but not enough to volunteer. Carl had his hand raised and was ready to go. He, apparently, hadn't changed.

"We decided to talk about something already discussed in the other books," Carl said, "to tie the books together. Family."

I saw Ari elbow Jessica.

"Okay, Carl, I'm interested. Take it *away*," Mrs. Gaarder said. She closed her eyes and leaned back in her chair like she was going to fall asleep, but we knew she wouldn't.

"We all know the basic story. Leslie is the new kid in Jess's fifth-grade class, and also his new neighbor." Sounded a bit too familiar. "They become best friends pretty quickly." Okay, maybe not that familiar. "The two of them use a rope to swing across a creek into Terabithia, a fantasy world they created to escape their real world." If only. "One day Leslie goes alone, the rope swing breaks, and Leslie dies."

He said it in one breath like he was telling us the facts and not thinking about the words.

He paused, and Mrs. Gaarder opened her eyes to check on him. See, she'd never fall asleep.

"They loved Terabithia because it was the place they had invented to get away from it all. It started as an escape from their bully, Janice. But then it became so much more. It became the place they could control everything when things in their real life became uncontrollable. And what's more uncontrollable than family?"

Mrs. Gaarder settled back again, and Carl continued. "Jess's family doesn't understand him, and Leslie's family ignores her. Unless they're done with their work, that is."

Carl crossed and uncrossed his arms. "Today we wanted to discuss the things we do because of family. Pretending to have fun at a place like Camp Green Lake; running away from home; creating a whole fantasy world. What is it about family that makes us do strange things?"

Mrs. Gaarder stepped in. "That's a very complicated question, Carl. I think this class is up to the task. Sometimes family members are similar, and sometimes they're different. Is it only when they're different that it makes us do—as you put it, strange things?"

Someone raised their hand. "In most families I know, everyone is kind of the same. Maybe families force themselves to be similar—so they don't have to create a whole imaginary world to escape."

Jack spoke up without waiting to be called on. "That's

the dumbest thing I've ever heard."

"Jack, care to rephrase that?"

"Well, some people have terrible family. Like, truly awful family. What she's saying is that it's not worth being better. That they should continue being awful to fit in."

Mrs. Gaarder tried leaning to the side so we could see her behind Carl. "I think what they're saying is there's a tendency to be like your family, but it doesn't mean you can't do anything about *it*."

I thought about how my uncle and I were so similar. I thought about his obituary, how no one remembered him with any meaningful detail. I liked how I reminded everyone of my uncle. But I also wanted people to say more than "He was happy to have others in the limelight" when it came to my obituary. Morbid, yes. Pathetic, a little. But honest.

Mrs. Gaarder walked out from behind her desk and stood next to Carl. She was still wrapped in the shawl, like a standing burrito. I remembered that shawl from a few years ago. Sara and I had been promised faloodas from the Indian store in exchange for quiet while Mom picked it out. We would have waited through anything for a falooda. I liked mine pink, piled high with syrups and nuts and clear noodles, but that day Mom took forever. She was buying a shawl to send Dad's friend for her birthday, and not in a million years would I have guessed I'd see that shawl again.

Carl led the rest of the class through a discussion about the complexities of family. A detailed discussion. A very detailed discussion. Would I call it boring? Nah, Carl was too good a friend.

CHAPTER
FIFTY

"Ahmed, do you mind staying *behind*," Mrs. Gaarder asked, "for a couple of minutes?"

We stood together waiting for the last person to leave before she closed the door and gestured for me to sit across from her. She was still clutching her shawl around her.

"So . . ."

"So," I replied.

"I wanted to check in and see how you're doing, Ahmed. You've had a lot to deal with."

She was right: I had a lot to deal with, and I was also teaching myself how to deal with it. I had a plan brewing. *Percolating.*

I glanced at the clock. I was going to be late for math.

"In all my years teaching I've never had a student go through something like that. There's no harm in asking for help, you know."

"Like how you helped me when you sent me chasing through those old school newspapers for no reason?" I was trying to change the topic and sound like I didn't care about those useless hours spent in the library. I may have sounded rude instead.

"Wait, you didn't find anything useful in those papers, Ahmed?"

I checked the clock again. I was definitely going to be late. The math teacher liked to make us stand in the front and explain to everyone why we were late. I hated that.

"Well, not nothing. I found a photo and a couple of little things. Mom showed me my uncle's obituary too."

She took her own sweet time to reply. If she really wanted to help, she could speed things along.

"I wrote that obituary, you know."

I assumed it was written by a teacher, by someone who didn't really know him. "You did?"

"Writing that was the hardest thing I've ever done." She bit her bottom lip and pushed her glasses up.

"Then why was it so short? So generic?"

She laughed with her head tilted back. "Is that how it comes across? I felt like I put my whole heart into it. I wanted everyone to know the Mohammed I knew. The guy who, even when he knew the answer or knew how to do something, let someone else take the glory. I wanted everyone to remember how he was always calm even when everyone else was not. I wanted everyone to know that we'd miss him."

I guess the obituary did say all of that.

"You know, your uncle was so infuriating," she said with a laugh.

"He was?"

"Oh yeah, I even nicknamed him Grumpy Old Man." She waited for it to sink in. "And, Ahmed, I wasn't trying to send you on a wild-goose chase. With your dad being in the hospital, I thought you needed a distraction. A diversion."

The first video camera I bought was too complicated for me. It had too many buttons and dials and lights, and Dad had warned me it was going to be tough to use, but I bought it anyway. He was right. I couldn't find the right dial to focus everything and was too proud to ask for help. For weeks I recorded blurry scenes and people. When I finally learned how to bring it into focus, to make all those blurry colors sharp and crisp, everything made sense. Mrs. Gaarder's words did the same for me.

"My uncle was Grumpy Old Man? He wrote that advice column in the school newspaper?"

Mrs. Gaarder smiled and nodded.

Maybe I had known all along.

CHAPTER
FIFTY-ONE

I'm calling an emergency meeting. We need to borrow the buzzers from Media Club, Ahmed, make it happen.

The end of the year was only making Jessica more tightly wound, and emergency meeting was no longer an unusual text for me to wake up to. The buzzer thing was new.

Three tables were set up to face each other in the cafeteria. "I spoke to some of the eighth graders who've lost to Mrs. Gaarder before, and getting to the buzzer is one of the reasons she always wins. I thought we should practice." She took the buzzers from me and set them on the tables.

At the beginning of the school year, I would have argued. Now I knew better. So did Ari and Jack. We showed up without a fight. In fact, Jack seemed to have lost his fight in general. I wouldn't say he was being nice, but he seemed to avoid me. I considered putting my plan on pause. Maybe I didn't need it. It felt good to know I had the upper hand, even though I wasn't an upper hand sort of guy.

"Ready?" she asked, trying out Mrs. Gaarder's voice. "What month is this?"

We looked at each other, confused. Did she forget the month, or was this our question? Ari finally rang his buzzer. "Umm, May."

"You got it."

"But why?" I asked.

"This is buzzer practice, plain and simple. We're focusing on one thing—using the buzzer effectively. It's not about the material today."

Ari and Jack didn't seem bothered by this exercise, like I was. "Wait, we woke up early so we could practice pressing a little button?"

She didn't answer. "Next question. What is the first name of your English teacher?"

Jack had his finger on the buzzer before I could move. "Janet."

"Great reaction time, Jack, that's what I'm talking about." She pointed at Jack for us to see, like we weren't sitting right next to him.

"Third question. What is my middle name?"

Ari's hand twitched, ready to answer, before resting it back in his lap. None of us moved. We must have looked strange to the guy dragging his backpack into the cafeteria.

"Good response. I wanted to make sure you don't get trigger-happy." She flipped to the next page of questions. "I don't have a middle name."

Who was going to tell Jessica she had completely lost it? I looked around. Apparently, none of us.

"Next question. On Connect, our school app, which student has the most friends and followers?"

Jack got to the buzzer first. "Well, I can definitely tell you who has the least followers," he answered, looking at me with a smirk.

I pressed my buzzer and held it down so it made an annoyingly long screech. Even if I didn't want the upper hand, I was definitely not going to let Jack take it back. Ever.

"I object." I released the buzzer.

"Not surprised," Jack replied.

"On what grounds?" Jessica asked.

"It's a trick question."

"Umm, no, it really isn't."

"Umm, yeah, it really is."

"Explain."

"Well, some people who we think have a lot of friends on Connect actually don't. They have burner accounts and use their hacking skills to change profile photos, Photoshop pictures, and even to pretend like they have a lot of—"

"This practice is a total waste of time. I'm out of here." Jack stood quickly, and the sound of his chair falling rattled through the cafeteria.

Nice to know my plan could work.

CHAPTER
FIFTY-TWO

I finally had enough footage of Jack to edit into one seamless video. I reminded myself that the difference between the photo Jack used to torture me and the video I was going to use to return the favor was simple. Mine was real. No Photoshop required.

I watched the video for the hundredth time. It felt like it was too much, and like it wasn't enough at the same time.

A video spliced together left room for doubt. If I was going to go through with this, there could be no room for doubt. I needed live footage.

That became the most complicated step in my plan.

For the lucky few, opportunities presented themselves, but for the rest of us, they had to be created. I had seen Stanley in *Holes* do it, Claudia from *Mixed-Up Files* do it, and Jess in *Bridge to Terabithia* do it. And I did it too.

That morning I went out of my way to make Jack notice me on the bus. I sat within earshot of him and started a very loud conversation with the poor kid sitting next to me who had no idea what was going on.

"Man, my little sister was so excited this morning. She got this flyer in the mail about a contest on a radio station. The winner gets private dance lessons from Kit Natcher. You've heard of Kit, right? He's the one who choreographs and teaches all the stars their dance moves."

I waited to see if Jack took the bait. He did. I saw him stop fidgeting and press his back against his seat to hear me better. Once he settled down, I continued.

"Yeah, she couldn't believe it. Apparently, if you're able to answer some questions about Kit, you get to meet him and learn some of his dance moves."

I didn't know the name of the kid who was sitting next to me, but he looked very confused.

"I don't know what kind of idiots likes those synchronized dance moves. Look at this flyer—what kind of person would be a fan? Besides my little sister, I mean."

And I left it at that.

When the bus got to school, I pretended to trip right in front of Jack. Tripping is something I'm good at.

Books, backpack, flyer, and I went flying through the air. I picked up the books. I picked up the backpack. I picked up myself. The flyer I left behind.

I turned around in time to see Jack shoving the flyer into his pocket. Step one complete.

CHAPTER
FIFTY-THREE

"I thought we'd do things slightly differently today," Mrs. Gaarder said. She moved the toddler heads in the maze. All of us pushing and shoving from our seats to see. We stayed in first place. Jessica let out a yelp. Very un-Jessica-like. For a contest I hadn't cared about all year long, I almost let out a yelp too.

"As usual, I have three questions, and I want each of you to answer one in essay form. Today I'm giving you the option to discuss the questions with your group. Or you can start writing your essays without a discussion." A few people groaned. "Which also means you won't have to do your essays at home." The same few people whooped.

"I didn't want to finish talking about *Terabithia* without hearing your thoughts on what I feel is the most important theme of the book."

"Death?" someone asked.

Mrs. Gaarder shook her head no.

"Friendship. In fact, why don't we make that the first question?" She held up her index finger. "Write them down.

"Question one. Why does Mrs. Gaarder feel—because this is arguable, I'll admit—that friendship is a more important theme than death?"

As I wrote the words down, I wasn't sure I agreed with her.

I raised my hand. "What if we disagree with you?"

She still had her index finger raised. "Well, the question is why *I*," she said, using that index finger to point at herself, "think friendship is more important. You don't have to agree with me. You have to argue my case."

One of the girls started to talk. "I think Mrs. Gaarder is right." Suck-up. "Leslie's friendship had a much bigger impact on Jess's life than her death did."

Mrs. Gaarder nodded at her. "I totally agree." She raised a second finger.

"Question two. How was Leslie a good friend to Jess? I want examples from the book."

This one was easy. Leslie taught Jess to use his imagination, to be himself, to stick up to the bully, to find his courage.

"And how was Jess a good friend to Leslie?"

I'd have to think about that one a little more.

"And finally, question three." She raised her hand above her head, three fingers raised. "Mrs. Myers and Miss Edmunds have very different reputations at their school. Why do you think the author did that? Why do you think Mrs. Myers was so unlikable?"

She lowered her arm and walked back to her chair. "As always, I will do the assignment, too, and post my answers on Connect once the deadline has passed."

The room was quiet except for slow clacking on keyboards. I guess no one preferred to discuss. Why was Mrs. Myers so unlikable? I tapped my eraser against my paper in a steady beat. There's no real reason to make someone unlikable. *Tap, tap, tap.* When we find out her husband had died, it sort of explained why she was always in a bad mood. *Tap, tap, tap.* She wasn't in a bad mood with Leslie, so was it the students that drove her into a bad mood? In the end, she was the only one who taught Jess how to cope with Leslie's death and gave him permission to keep Leslie's memory alive. *Tap, tap, tap.* Maybe the author was telling us we can learn things from the most unexpected places? *Tap, tap.*

Jessica grabbed my pencil, gave me a dirty look, and put it on my table.

Some people had no issues with being unlikable, I guess.

CHAPTER
FIFTY-FOUR

My plan to get back at Jack was coming together with little effort. I guess I had found my true calling. Revenge.

Jack had my flyer. My flyer had an email on it. I waited for Jack to write. The only person invited to this email party.

He took the bait, and that evening I replied.

Dear Jack,

We are so excited to inform you that you are a finalist for the special meet and greet with Kit Natcher! This could be a once-in-a-lifetime experience for you and a friend. We have one more step to help weed out the wannabe fans from the die-hard ones. Be ready to answer some questions about Kit and his career, Thursday morning at 8:30

a.m. Any true fan should be able to answer them.

We ask two things of you: 1. You must answer your phone and 2. You must have a phone or device by which you can send live video.

Talk to you then, and best of luck!

Sincerely,

The staff of KS53.5

It was already Wednesday. I had a lot to do.

First, I had to make sure I was the one in charge of running Morning Report that Thursday. That was easy enough.

Second, I had to set up our radio and video devices to pick up the frequency of his Noguchi headphones. Also not a problem.

Third, I had to turn on his headphones so it would be able to transmit. That would be a little more difficult.

All I had to do was press the green and yellow buttons together three times on the side of his headphones, but it was a question of access. Jack wasn't going to let me play around with his headphones, after all. I waited for Jack to put his headphones down, if only for a second. I watched him like a hawk and followed him like a bloodhound. I had to be swift and efficient, generally not words used to describe me.

The vice principal waved him to the front of the

cafeteria, and Jack pulled his headphones down around his neck before going over. Of all the days to enforce the rule about no technology at school, of course he chose this one. Jack handed his headphones to the vice principal.

If Jack didn't have his headphones tomorrow at the time of the phone call, the whole plan would fall apart. I followed the vice principal out of the cafeteria. Vice Principal Daniels was a strange guy. We wouldn't see him for weeks, and then he was everywhere at once, with his ridiculous mustache and bad comb-over and sarcastic humor. I kept a ten-foot distance between us and watched him at work. He must have woken up on the wrong side of the bed. He made one girl take a hat off and hand it to him, took an electronic game from another, and confiscated a cell phone from someone else. "Pick it up from my office at the end of the day," he said. And by the time he left the cafeteria, he had a pile of contraband items. He made his way back to his office, and in his green jacket he looked like a leprechaun with a too-heavy pot of gold.

It was still lunchtime, but I found myself following him to his office. I knew it was my last chance to get to Jack's headphones. I knocked on Mr. Daniels's door and pushed it open before he could answer. He closed a big drawer behind his desk before turning around. He must have stashed his pot of gold in there.

"Mr. Daniels," I started, but honestly didn't know where I was going with this. "Ummm . . . you should head back to the cafeteria right away."

"And tell me, Ahmed, why I'd want to do that."

He knew my name?

"Looks like a food fight was breaking out, and it was taking a bad turn," I replied. I couldn't believe how easily it came to me. Not the slightest hesitation in my voice.

Of course he knew my name. It wasn't long ago that I was standing in the conference room next door with two cops by my side.

"Ah, a snitch. Every vice principal's dream come true." And he was out the door.

I shut the door behind him and ran to the drawer he had closed. I could feel my heart pounding in my throat. Swift and efficient, I told myself. I opened the drawer. It was heavy, and I had to pull hard to make it move. It was full of folders and files but nothing else. Row after row of color-coded folders divided by grade and alphabetically by name. I opened the next and then the next, the sweaty imprints of my hands drying quickly on each metallic drawer. Aziz was at the front, and I considered reading it, but I knew what it would have to say. High test scores, low grades. Pages of analysis trying to explain why.

Another folder was way more interesting to me.

Someone I had been eavesdropping on for days, someone I had been videotaping for weeks, someone I had been avoiding for months.

Jack.

I shouldn't read it.

It wouldn't be right.

I could get in serious trouble.

I opened the folder.

There were the usual test scores and emergency contact numbers, but there was also something else. There was a profile of Jack. A summary written by a therapist. Mandated by court.

I froze when I heard voices in the front office as they returned from lunch. I looked around for an escape, but there were no windows and no other doors. What's the point of being vice principal if you couldn't get an office with a window?

Mr. Daniels was talking about his summer plans to visit New York City, his words interrupted by the pounding in my ears. Ellis . . . Times Square . . . bridge. The doorknob turned, but with nowhere to run, I rushed to sit in the chair facing his desk. I turned my head, and we were looking right at each other.

"What do you think you're doing in here?"

"Oh, I thought you wanted me to wait here until you got back. You didn't?" I asked innocently.

"Can you think of one good reason why I would want that?" he shot back.

"Umm . . . I guess not." I tried to sound as casual as possible. Walking out, I saw the headphones, hat, game, phone, and other confiscated items on a bookshelf behind the door. I held the door in my left hand, reached above the cabinet, and pressed the buttons on the headphones like I had seen them do on the YouTube video. I did it all while the vice principal was standing right in front of me.

"What exactly are you doing?" he asked.

"Oh, nothing. I thought that was my deck of cards up there," I answered. He looked me up and down. There were sweat stains on the front of my shirt, my face felt hot, and my hair was sticking to the sides of my face. He looked at my hands, but they were empty.

"You can pick it up at the end of the school day like everyone else, Ahmed. And by the way, there was no food fight in the cafeteria. The only thing worse than a snitch is a bad one. Don't be late for class."

I was out before he could finish his sentence.

Step two complete.

CHAPTER
FIFTY-FIVE

The class was squeezed together outside Mrs. Gaarder's door when I got there, elbowing and shoving to get the best view through the glass on the side of the closed door.

"What's going on?" I asked.

Carl was a head shorter than everyone else and had no chance of getting a look. "Since our school was the first to distribute laptops to every student, they're featuring us in a news report about the use of technology in schools. They're interviewing Mrs. Gaarder and may interview some of her students . . ."

"And they're doing it during our class," gum-smacking girl explained while she and her friends stood in a circle putting on lipstick and holding mirrors for each other while they fixed their hair. "Which means *we* are going to be on TV!"

I wiped new sweat that seemed to still be forming on my forehead. I wanted to sit in class and let my heart rate return to normal. So, of course, there was going to be a news crew in our classroom.

"Of course there's going to be a news crew in our classroom today," Carl said. "I'm missing most of class for a dentist appointment." I wished we could switch places.

The door opened, and the entire class pushed through into an unnaturally bright light. "Watch your step," a gruff voice warned. There was a roll of wire like the trunk of a tree running across the middle of the floor, breaking off into branches everywhere. I waited for my eyes to adjust to the brightness. Mrs. Gaarder was in the corner talking to a woman in a red suit who was trying to balance on shoes that were too high and too pointy. A man with an enormous video camera on his shoulder adjusted the lights on the floor. Any other day I would have stared at the camera, envious of all it could do. "Watch your step," he yelled again. We found our way to chairs pushed into odd sections of the room, breaking us into groups we weren't accustomed to.

Mrs. Gaarder stepped over the tree trunk. "Okay, guys," she said to us, "things are a little different today. We'll let these lovely people do their job, and then we'll get on with ours, *okay*?"

The lady in the suit wobbled to the front of the class

next to Mrs. Gaarder, balancing like a stilt walker. "Hello, children." Children? "My name is June Page, from the KTR3 evening news. I'm sure you've heard of me." I had not. "Word has gotten around that Mrs. Gaarder is an amazing teacher." Mrs. Gaarder turned pink and looked down at her shoes. "We're here to see whether technology in the classroom helps her or gets in the way." Mrs. Gaarder fiddled with the ring on her finger. "I know it can get a little overwhelming in here, so if any of you need a break, just raise your hand." Mrs. Gaarder raised her hand, and even the cameraman laughed. "Not you, Mrs. Gaarder."

Separated from our usual groups, we felt unsettled and out of place. *Untethered*. "We generally like to tape a section of how your day normally looks. Why don't you guys pretend we're not here?" Easier said than done.

"Umm, okay." Mrs. Gaarder walked to the middle of the room and tried to get her bearings. "Who wants to give it a try and start the discussion today?" She looked at me, but I looked at my lap. She turned a quarter circle and looked at Carl's spot since he could always be counted on to come through. But it was already empty. Even the lipstick girls only half raised their hands before putting them back down.

The reporter stepped forward, placing a hand on Mrs.

Gaarder's shoulder—for balance, I think. "I know it can feel awkward. Maybe we can talk to some of you one-on-one and get an idea of what you like about technology in the classroom and what you don't." She took an unsteady step toward Mrs. Gaarder. "We can set up in the corner there and interview a few kids, if that's okay with you?"

One of the lipstick girls had her hand raised so high, I thought she would dislocate her arm. "I have some great thoughts on how we use technology," she said. I don't think she'd be able to tell the difference between a USB and an HDMI if her life depended on it.

"Maybe Mrs. Gaarder could suggest a few students she thinks would be the most help," June Page suggested.

Mrs. Gaarder looked around the room. "I think you might want to start with someone from Media Club." She looked at me.

"Great idea, Mrs. Gaarder. I'm sure Carl would do a great job," I volunteered. The brown kid talking about technology seemed a little too on the nose.

Mrs. Gaarder looked at the clock. "Yes, except Carl is already gone. What do you think, Ahmed? Ready for the challenge?"

I looked at the corner they had set up. "Umm, I guess."

"Let's try to salvage some of this day, shall we? Let's get back to our book while they work on their interviews."

I sat opposite June Page while she asked me a zillion questions, one after the other, often not pausing for my answer. Questions about Morning Report, Connect, homework assignments online, smartboards, test taking on computers.

Talking about things I actually understood made it easy to answer, but I was glad to be done.

"Who's next?" the reporter asked.

A few hands went up.

"Jack is our biggest user of Connect. He could be next," Mrs. Gaarder said. He flashed a big smile before taking the spot I had left.

When I returned to my chair, the girl who stumbled and barely made it through her presentation of *From the Mixed-Up Files* was raising her hand to speak. Nooooooooooooo. We had only a few classes left until the end of the year. She could have kept her hand down and sneaked past without a disastrous repeat performance. Some people love pain, I guess.

She pulled her hair back and tucked it behind both ears. Here we go.

"I really loved the whole idea of Terabithia, the land. In the beginning it was an escape for Jess and Leslie. An escape from everything they disliked or was difficult in their daily life."

She held index cards this time and squared them to be perfectly lined up.

"When they were in Terabithia, they felt like they could do anything. After a while that feeling of being invincible leaked into their real word as well. Soon they were able to fight their real problems just like they fought their fake ones."

We were interrupted by the reporter again. "I think we'll have time for one more person."

Lipstick girl looked so eager and excited. "Why don't you go ahead?" Mrs. Gaarder asked.

"Hana," Mrs. Gaarder said. So that was her name. "Sorry about the interruption. Continue."

She cleared her throat. She was different from the last time. She was clear and confident. She wasn't looking around with desperation, hoping for someone to rescue her.

"I think," she continued, "when they practiced ridding their enemies in the pretend world, they gained the confidence to tackle their problems in the real one."

"I couldn't agree with you more," Mrs. Gaarder said. "Sometimes when we tell ourselves we can do something, we can."

Hana couldn't have looked more pleased. Jessica kicked me from behind. "Say something, man. Get in there. We need to keep our points."

Like a knee responding to a doctor's reflex hammer, my hand shot up from Jessica's kick.

"You have something to add, Ahmed?" Mrs Gaarder asked.

"Well, I do agree with Hana." I swear I could hear the sound of Jessica's eyeballs scraping against her eye sockets as she rolled them. "What I wanted to add is that even though Terabithia was in Jess's life for a short time, it made a huge impact. They were best friends for less than the school year, but Jess was changed forever." I had known my uncle even less.

"And how do we know that Jess was changed forever?" Mrs. Gaarder asked.

"Because he took his little sister to Terabithia after Leslie died."

"So?"

"Leslie was the one who was creative and imaginative enough to come up with Terabithia. But he didn't let Terabithia die with Leslie. He brought it back for his little sister. He wanted to pass on what he learned."

It was silent in the room as we thought about Leslie's death and the loss of a best friend. Mrs. Gaarder whispered so she wouldn't interrupt the silence. "And what do you think he learned in Terabithia?"

I knew it. Because I had learned the same thing from someone who had died too.

"To be yourself."

The bell rang, jarring us back from Terabithia into the classroom, and we carefully picked our way over the trunk of wires, out of the camera lights, and back to the real world.

CHAPTER
FIFTY-SIX

Like the chessboard perpetually set up in my living room, the pieces of my plan were lined up and ready to go. The evil genius in me wanted to rub my hands together and laugh: "MWA-HA-HA." The not-so-evil genius in me felt uncomfortable, like my T-shirt was too tight around the neck. I looked at my uncle's photo above my locker, and he was frowning.

Sofie was reading the news for the day, and she began with the weather before going through the lunch specials. I watched the clock, and the moment the minute hand clicked to 8:30, I placed the call. With his headphones turned on, any call Jack received could be transmitted live on Morning Report. The phone rang once, twice, a third time, before going to voice mail.

I double-checked the number and called again. It rang

once, twice, then "Hello?" It was Jack, out of breath and squeaky voiced.

"This is KS95.3. Jack Hanson? Please hold."

Sofie was about to tell the joke she had rehearsed. I hit mute, so her mouth was moving but she had no idea her words weren't being heard. It wasn't a very funny joke, so technically I was doing her a favor. Jack stayed on hold. I knew what I was going to say. "Good morning, Cedar Valley Middle School. Do we have a treat for you today!"

My hand hesitated over the switch. This was my last chance to spare Jack, even if he had never spared me. I thought about Jess and Leslie taking revenge on their bully. Yes, it felt good. But only for a little while.

I thought about what I read in Jack's school folder. It made sense why Jack was the only one at the pep rally without a parent, why his house was the only one not lit up for Christmas, why he talked about not wanting to be like his awful family in classroom discussions.

When Jack's parents got divorced, his dad moved across the country and didn't think Jack should change schools. His mom traveled for work and couldn't care for Jack. So they fought it out in court.

But they were not fighting because they wanted him. They were fighting because they didn't want him.

I can't imagine how that must have felt.

I might have turned out a jerk too.

But I didn't. And I had a lot going on in my life, didn't I? And a lot of that was brought on by Jack, wasn't it? And he deserved it, didn't he?

Weeks of hard work at my fingertips. All I had to do was flip a switch.

I would introduce Jack as the Student of the Month. I had a special video made, an editing masterpiece. It had bits of Jack bullying the Chosen Few in the halls spliced together with video of him dancing. I was giving everyone a chance to hate him or make fun of him.

But first, to make sure there was no question of whether the photos were real, I was going to capture him live for the whole school to see. All that stood between me and the moment was flipping that switch.

My stomach knotted. My voice, distorted by an app, helped me pretend someone else was making the call.

"Jack Hanson. We at KS95.3 are huge fans of Kit Natcher. You must be, too, right?"

"Definitely. The biggest."

"Tell us, Jack, what makes you a fan?" I hate to admit it, but I was enjoying myself. It was nice to be able to speak to him when he didn't know who I was.

"I love the way he breaks down each move so it's easy

to learn. And I love the way he puts together moves that I wouldn't have thought of putting together. He's genius."

He was enjoying it too.

"Our contest, today, Jack, is one Kit himself came up with."

"He did?" I could hear the smile in his voice.

"Kit thinks a true fan would know the moves from his latest dance. He thinks a true fan would have no problem proving it. Are you a true fan, Jack?"

There was a pause, but not for long. "Totally. The biggest."

I turned on the video feed. "Okay, Jack, it's time for you to turn on your camera and prove it."

And right there, on the little screen in front of me, Jack started the dance moves I had seen him practice. He was completely immersed. He put his arms in the air like he was throwing an invisible basketball. He bent at the waist, he turned, he swayed.

He was actually pretty good. If I had those moves, I wouldn't mind being broadcast across the school. But Jack minded, and that's why it could work.

I hung up the phone without ending the conversation. I had what I needed.

CHAPTER
FIFTY-SEVEN

I got to class before Jack. I had pictured this moment for weeks. The whole class, the whole school, erupting into laughter.

Jack walked in looking a little confused, but class began as if nothing unusual had happened. Because it hadn't.

When my hand hovered over that switch and I was given one final chance to change my mind, I took it.

I could follow him and listen to him, but I could never be him. And I didn't want to be. It's like my uncle, the Grumpy Old Man, told me. You be you.

I was done pretending to be anyone other than myself, and myself was a little Jess, and a little Claudia, and a little Stanley.

And like Jess when he comforted their bully, maybe

courage is also knowing when not to fight.

And like Claudia, maybe knowing a secret without sharing it is enough.

And like Stanley, maybe I could be good and good things would happen to me.

"What are you staring at, idiot?" Jack snarled at me.

Maybe not.

CHAPTER
FIFTY-EIGHT

"Do you even know where you're going, Dad?"

He smiled and stroked his chin, making a scratching sound. His stubble was growing in again, but there was more gray in it than I remembered. "This was my town, son, I'd know where I was going with my eyes closed."

Dad had picked me up from school on Mom's orders. We were meeting her and Sara, but he was a little sketchy on exactly where. "Let's get some music going, shall we?" Dad asked.

"Play Bilal's playlist," he spoke into the car's music system. He spoke loud and slow, pronouncing it *Bilayyyl*. "Calling Bill's Ale house," the car replied. "End call," he yelled, "end call!" I couldn't help but laugh.

"These silly voice-activated machines weren't built

to recognize any names that don't sound like Mark or Susan."

"Play Bilal's playlist." He tried again, speaking louder and slower, and pronouncing it *Bye-layl* this time. "Sorry," the computer voice apologized, "Byvail not found." We both laughed this time.

I took over for him. "Play Bilal's playlist," I said. Prince's "Kiss" filled our car.

"I guess you've got the touch I never had, Ahmed. I remember fiddling with my Walkman for hours as a kid, trying to get it to work. Mohammed would barely touch it, and like a miracle it would start."

"I know, I know. I remind you of him."

"And I'm so glad you do. You have his curls, and his smile, and his sarcastic sense of humor. But more importantly, Ahmed, you have his good heart. Both of you have this quiet strength. I wish I had that."

Like what Mrs. Gaarder said in her obituary.

I thought of all the things I had done that year that would have changed Dad's mind. I had tried changing who I was. I had considered revenge. Neither sounded like quiet strength or a good heart.

"I don't think I'm as good as you think I am, Dad. Not as good as your brother."

Of course Mom had told Dad about Jack framing me,

but in the car that day, my version of the story came tumbling out. How Jack had picked on me, how he had taped my picture everywhere, how he had made my life miserable, and how I had tried to do the same to him.

"And what stopped you from going through with it?"

"I don't know, Dad. It wasn't for me, that's all." And that was the truth.

We had pulled into a parking lot.

"But you didn't go through with it, Ahmed. And that's the difference."

"But barely, Dad. I came so close."

Dad ruffled my hair and pulled me in to inhale the top of my head.

"Barely, Ahmed, is what makes the difference between a good guy and a great guy."

I didn't feel like a good guy, and I definitely didn't feel like a great guy.

"Where did you say we were supposed to go, Dad? This doesn't look right." He checked the folded piece of paper that was in his front pocket.

"No, this is the right address. Let's go see."

He knocked on the door, but no one answered. He knocked louder.

I pushed the door hard and it opened. "Door's open, Dad."

Lights turned on, and the crowd inside screamed, "Surprise!" in unison. Everyone was there exactly as planned. Mom, and Sara, and Mrs. Gaarder, and all the aunties and uncles, and the nurses from the hospital, and Carl, and Ari, and Jessica. A banner ran across the wall that read, "Happy Birthday, Bilal" in green and red, and it looked so much happier than when it was scribbled on a whiteboard in a hospital room.

The evening passed with music, and food, and cake, and laughter, and when everyone said they couldn't have another cup of payasam or another bite of ras malai, it was time for presents. Dad sat in the folding chair next to the table covered with presents of different sizes and shapes, opening them one at a time. Mom gave him a journal, to write down all the wonderful memories we have yet to make, she said, and everyone clapped. Sara gave him a half-painted picture of our family and a green knitted coaster that had started out as a sweater, and everyone said how cute. The nurses gave him a hospital gown—in case you missed us, they said—and everyone laughed.

Finally it was time for him to open my gift. I had worked hard on it. You could say I worked on it all year. He untied the purple ribbon delicately and picked at the tape. Sara couldn't stand it, ripping the paper off for him. It was a leather-bound book. There was no title along the side, and no table of contents in the front. I had learned sometimes it was fun not to know what you were looking for.

"Dear Grumpy Old Man," it said on the first page, and between the bound leather was a copy of every piece he had written.

No one in that room knew what was in that book. But I did. And Dad did. And that was plenty.

CHAPTER
FIFTY-NINE

"So, did you see it?" Carl asked.

"See what?"

"You didn't see it? Man, it was glorious. You're going to love it."

All morning I had noticed people huddled around their phones, laughing. Everyone but me. I assumed it was another joke I wasn't part of. After the ballet photo fiasco, any joke I wasn't part of was a good joke.

Carl tried to play the video on his phone. At the table next to mine, neck brace guy was talking to his friends, not scarfing his lunch down in a teacher's room. His brace was out in all its glory.

"What's going on?"

Carl was shaking his phone in frustration. "The school's news piece on technology, that's what's going on. They televised it last night. You've got to see it."

The video wouldn't load.

James, from Media Club, clapped to get our attention. "Hey, could everyone turn off their phones? The cafeteria Wi-Fi doesn't have the bandwidth for all of you at the same time. I know what you want to watch. I'm hooking it up to the screen here, but you've got to turn off your phones."

"Okay, Ahmed, you're going to love this. It's epic."

June Page and her red suit filled the screen, with Mrs. Gaarder barely visible by her side. If I hadn't been there myself, I wouldn't have noticed the slight shake as she tried her best to stay upright on those heels.

"I'm here today with Ms. Janet Gaarder, sixth-grade Language Arts teacher, to talk about how she's incorporated technology into her classroom at Cedar Valley Middle School."

Mrs. Gaarder smiled. The camera panned the classroom, and someone yelled, "Hey, there's me!" as they identified themselves.

Gum girl was on screen, twirling her hair, and the caption under her read "sixth-grade student." "Technology is, like, just the best. It's, like, totally cool."

June Page's voice spoke over the video. "Cedar Valley Middle School has embraced technology in the classroom, and sometimes it can be a real help."

Suddenly I was on-screen. "Ahmed Aziz, sixth-grade student, member of Media Club," it said. "What I love about incorporating technology is how it makes things easier. I can check my homework assignments from anywhere, don't have to carry heavy books from class to class, and since we can look up class lessons anytime, I can focus on the discussions in class instead of worrying about taking notes." I looked pretty good, and I sounded pretty good. I didn't remember feeling that way. And like my dad in that newspaper photo, my name was actually in the caption.

June Page was back on-screen. "Of course, there's always a downside." June Page was interviewing the principal, his computer behind him. "Being the principal through this transition toward technology in every classroom, what would you say has been the biggest hurdle?"

The principal was not my favorite person, and when he smiled it irritated me.

"Staying ahead of the kids has to be the toughest thing. The students tend to be much better with technology in general, and staying one step ahead of them is probably the biggest challenge."

June Page directed the microphone toward herself.

"What do you mean exactly?"

"For example, I was just dealing with something now," he said, pointing to the computer screen behind him. "The students are encouraged to use the platform Connect instead of other social media because we know it's safer." June Page nodded. "Having the most friends and followers is a big deal." June Page nodded again. "And we just found out one student hacked into our system to increase his stats and make it look like he had more followers than he did. Now imagine if they could do that with their grades and test scores as well."

The camera zoomed in on the principal as he spoke. The photo on his screen was blurry and fuzzy, hard to recognize if you didn't know him. But we all knew Jack. You know, because he had the most friends on Connect. Except he didn't.

I couldn't hear her sign off over the incredible laughter. Neck brace guy was laughing. "How pathetic do you have to be to pretend to have the most followers on the school website?"

I looked around for Jack, but he was nowhere to be seen. If he was, I'd tell him everything would be okay. After all, humiliation isn't so bad. It's definitely preferable to police interrogation. I would know. I had been through both.

CHAPTER
SIXTY

The last day of school was always a short day, which made me wonder, why bother? Why not end school the day before? We had only one class left: Language Arts with Mrs. Gaarder.

"What can I say that hasn't already been said?" Mrs. Gaarder asked. "It's been a fantastic ride with all of you this year. I learned a lot and hope you did as well."

I definitely had.

"Some of you lucky people will get to see me again next year." Someone let out an "Aww."

"I know. I know. Try to contain your excitement. Next year we will do a similar exercise using works by Shakespeare. We will read three plays and find relevance to our lives. Exciting, right?"

I knew she was trying to be funny, but actually, yes, it

did seem a little exciting.

"And now, the day you've all been waiting for. The brownies are ready. The lemonade is poured. The only question left unanswered is—ARE . . . YOU . . . SMARTER . . . THAN . . . MRS. GAARDER?"

The class cheered and clapped, like we had won a cruise to the Caribbean.

"But first, the reigning champion from last year will take a victory lap around the classroom." She picked up the little trophy, exaggerated the weight of it, lifted it over her head with one hand, holding the base between her index finger and thumb, and walked around the room. We booed when she put it back on her desk. "Jealousy, my friends, is not a pretty color on any of you.

"I'd like to introduce you to our very impartial and very smart judge. He may not know his regular verbs from his irregular, but he can solve a quadratic equation with his eyes closed. He was hand selected after an arduous process of weeding through all the teachers who had a free period at this time. He was the only one. Put your hands together for everyone's favorite math teacher . . . Mr. Jensen."

Mr. Jensen came through the door. He had a sticker on his jacket that said *Hello, my name is . . . Judge* and carried a small whiteboard and marker. He stroked his beard, pretended to twirl his mustache, and sat on the stool that was left for him before turning his back to the class. Half the class cheered, and the other half booed.

"There are two rounds of competition. In the first, each group will present their case. We have a very high-tech solution to keeping Mr. Jensen impartial. He will keep his back turned. Arguing with the judge is grounds for immediate disqualification and possible withholding of brownies."

Mr. Jensen pretended to flex his muscles.

"In the first round, each group will present one major change or insight they've learned through this class. You will have a few minutes to discuss among yourselves before presenting. We will then add those points to what you already have," she said as she tilted her head to the maze on the board, "and the winning team will proceed to stage two. Clear?"

We could barely hear her as everyone started their discussions. Jessica pulled on my sleeve with an urgency more suited to telling me a tornado was coming or pulling me out of the path of a moving truck. "What have we got? What did we learn? Where are your notes?"

"Wow, Jessica, didn't know you could get any more anxious about that stupid little trophy."

"I'm with Jessica on this one. What do we have?" Ari

asked and gripped my other sleeve.

I released Jessica's hand from one side and did the same to Ari's. "Settle down, kids, settle down. You both need to chill. I've got this."

After all, there's no way anyone could have learned more than me through this class.

Jack didn't have a lot to say. He kept his head lowered, his voice down, and his chair a little distant.

But Mrs. Gaarder didn't give us much time. "Group one," she said, pulling a name out of a basket. "Carl's group, you're up."

Carl started to get up and sat back down. Mr. Always Prepared wasn't sure of himself. "Umm. I learned that you can't judge anything from its looks. In *Holes*, Zero and Stanley were the least likely to look like heroes. I'm pretty small, so I liked how the ones who looked unlikely to win, won," Carl said. "Being a hero has nothing to do with size."

I had to agree. Carl didn't even look small to me anymore. The whole class clapped, and someone whistled. Mr. Jensen pulled a marker out of his pocket, took the cap off with exaggerated effort, wrote on the whiteboard, and lifted it above his head for us to see.

"The judge has decreed 8.1," Mrs. Gaarder said. Carl sat down, and his group ruffled his hair until he smiled.

"Group two—are you ready to beat that?" Mrs. Gaarder asked, pointing to Hana's group.

Hana stood up. "I'd have to say what I learned was that sometimes if you pretend to have courage, you become courageous."

Mr. Jensen shrugged and gestured *more* with both his hands. The marker rolled off his lap, and he got up to get it.

"Well, when I first started the year, I'd never have considered joining the Drama Club. But I joined, I loved it, made so many friends out of it, and learned how to get over my fear of performing."

So *that's* what made the big difference between the first and second time she presented.

"It's like that kid in *Terabithia*. He was the king when he was in Terabithia. And so he learned to be powerful even when he swung back to reality on the rope swing."

Mr. Jensen wrote his score and lifted it over his head. "8.4," Mr. Jensen said.

Next up was cool guy. "We learned that it's not necessarily the destination, but the journey," he said. He wore a blue-striped shirt. He probably had a yacht waiting for him to sail around the world. "In *The Mixed-Up Files*, all Claudia wanted to do was run away. It wasn't what she was running away from or running to that was important. It was all the stuff she learned on the way. Sometimes it's nice to enjoy what's around you, you know?" I was wrong. He wasn't waiting to get on his yacht. He was meant to be on a surfboard on a beach somewhere.

Mr. Jensen held up his sign. "8.0."

"Okay, last group—it's your turn. Let's see what you've got."

I had been so wrapped up in everything that happened to me, I hadn't realized how the class had affected anyone else. I thought about all the things I had learned. I had learned that my experiences, no matter how difficult, made me stronger. I had learned that family doesn't mean you have to be related. I had learned that the most comfortable skin to be in is your own. But I couldn't find the words for all that.

I stood up. "Here it is. Friends and family are important, but they don't define you. You get to choose who you are. And you get to choose to become bigger and better. We saw it in all three books. Stanley chose to help his friend, and it helped his own situation. Claudia chose to keep a secret, and it helped her feel complete. Jess chose to honor Leslie's memory instead of forgetting her, and it would help his younger sister. Choose the right path, and good things will happen."

Mr. Jensen paused with marker in hand but finally wrote down a number. "For incorporating all three books . . . 8.5."

Mrs. Gaarder stood at her desk, calculator in hand. We were already in first place, and I was pretty sure that meant we'd won. But we waited patiently while she tapped numbers into her calculator. Like you needed a calculator to add those numbers. She walked to the front in an exaggeratedly slow pace. She slowly lifted her hand before turning to the class. "Maybe we should have a snack first?"

The whole class screamed, "Nooooooo!"

She turned back with a smile, picked up a toddler head, and moved it to the end of the maze. When she stepped out of the way, we saw whose it was.

Jessica and Ari pulled me into my chair. Jessica almost hugged me. Almost, because she hadn't completely lost her mind. She put her arm around my shoulders and patted my back. Ari and I fist-bumped.

"Okay, settle down. Everyone get a snack, and we'll reconvene for . . . ROUND TWO." Jack got swept up in the moment, and we even high-fived. I think he was going to be okay after all.

CHAPTER
SIXTY-ONE

There was a mad scramble for the snack line, and our group was mobbed, with everyone offering advice on how to beat Mrs. Gaarder. From how to get our fingers to move fast enough for the buzzer to not looking her straight in the eye. Dude, she's not Medusa.

Mr. Jensen and Mrs. Gaarder set tables up while we ate. He stood at the podium in between us. On one side was a single chair and desk, and on his other side were four chairs and one desk. Both desks had a buzzer on it.

"Contestants, take your seats," he said in his best game-show voice.

Mrs. Gaarder pretended to dust off her seat, sat down, cracked her knuckles in front of her, and squinted her eyes to stare at us.

We moved one of the chairs out of the way for Ari and

took our seats. Jessica was directly in front of the buzzer.

"There will be five questions today. The team that gets the first three right will be declared the winner. Are we ready to see if you

ARE

SMARTER

THAN

MRS. GAARDER?" he asked, echoing each word like a microphone gone bad.

"Question one. Hands off the table, Mrs. Gaarder. No cheating. In the book *Holes*, all the boys have nicknames. What is X-Ray's real name?"

Mrs. Gaarder rang the buzzer before Jessica even lifted her hand. "Rex," Mrs. Gaarder answered. "His name is Rex."

"We need a last name, too, Mrs. Gaarder," Mr. Jensen said.

Mrs. Gaarder leaned forward in her chair. "That's a trick question. He didn't have a last name."

Jessica rang the buzzer. "Washburn. His name is Rex Washburn."

Mr. Jensen walked to the board and put one tally mark for "Team Hopefuls," under our laminated toddler head on the board.

"That is correct. Question two. This is a two-part

question. You need to get both parts right. What is a palindrome? And part two, give us an example from one of the books."

Again, Mrs. Gaarder had the buzzer. She was like lightning. "A palindrome is a word that reads the same backward and forward. Stanley Yelnats is a palindrome."

Mr. Jensen put one tally under "Team Champion."

"It's a tie," he said, "and I don't need to be a math teacher to know that.

"Question three. In *Bridge to Terabithia*, what is Leslie's dad's jo—"

Ari was on the buzzer before the question was over. "A writer." Mr. Jensen paused, and Ari looked at us, bewildered. "A political writer."

"You are correct, but may I remind you that you're playing a dangerous game, sir. That could have been a two-part question, and you would have forfeited."

Jessica punched Ari on the shoulder.

"Question four. What was the nickname the kids had given their teacher, Mrs. Myers?"

I reached for the buzzer but had no clue and set it back down. We looked at each other. Was it something that started with *M*? Mrs. Gaarder coughed, pretended to blow on her nails, and then slowly pressed the buzzer. "Mr. Jensen, I don't condone students making up mean names for their teacher, but I believe the correct answer is Monster Mouth Myers."

"That is correct."

Mrs. Gaarder looked at us. "You guys want to call it a day? Should I pick up the trophy right now?"

"People don't usually trash-talk when they're tied, Mrs. Gaarder," Jessica replied.

"Tiebreaker question. This is a toughie. What food item inspired E. L. Konigsburg to write *From the Mixed-Up Files of Mrs. Basil E. Frankweiler*?"

Mrs. Gaarder picked up the buzzer, but then set it back down with a confused look on her face. "Food item?" she asked.

"No questions. Only answers, please," Mr. Jensen replied.

I picked up the buzzer. I coughed. I blew on my nails as Mrs. Gaarder had and pressed the buzzer.

"Yes, Team Hopefuls?"

"I believe the correct answer, Mr. Jensen," I said, "is popcorn."

"That is correct."

The entire class was on me in a second. Someone grabbed the trophy off the desk and pushed it into our hands. The four of us formed the front of the parade, and the rest followed. I got it. That pathetic little trophy felt like a really big deal.

We circled the room before Mrs. Gaarder opened the door. "Go ahead," she said, "take a lap."

The whole procession left the room, and we laughed, screamed, and whooped a full circle of the school. Students and teachers stuck their heads out of classrooms to hear what the noise was about, giving us a chance to yell out, "WE are smarter than Mrs. Gaarder! WE are smarter than Mrs. Gaarder!"

When we returned to the room, the class lined up in the front, and the four of us walked past, giving each person a chance to high-five us or pat our back or shake our hands. Like we were celebrities. And we grinned from ear to ear.

And I didn't have to fake it.

Because I had made it.

ACKNOWLEDGMENTS

Alyssa—because I don't know what made you pick my skeleton of a manuscript out of your slush pile, or what made you take the time to read it again, and again, and then again (after all, as my father pointed out, it's not Shakespeare), but I am eternally grateful.

Alexandra—because your attention to detail is unbelievable, and I'm so happy that my details are the ones to which you chose to pay attention. Thank you, thank you.

To the entire team at HarperCollins—because you made my book look this beautiful and polished, and because now no one has to know how much I struggle with basic grammar. And because David DeWitt and Shreya Devarakonda designed the beautiful cover that makes me smile every time I see it. And because Allison Weintraub answered every question and email, and never made me feel as clueless as I felt.

The Loft Literary Center—because there was a class for me when I was ready to start ("Your book starts here"—Mary Carroll Moore), and another when I was ready to revise it ("Planning your way through revisions"—Stephanie Watson), and another for all the steps in between.

My couch—because the moment I saw you at the Room and Board outlet, I knew. Three kids, three houses, and now one book later—I wasn't wrong.

Kara—because when we had dinner all those years ago and I said I wanted to be a writer you said, "So, write!" and then graciously invited me into your wonderful world of writing, and writers and retreats.

The Gandhis—because you always cheer me on, but also because you always have a spot set for me at your table for pani puri and jerk chicken and homemade Nutella ice cream.

Nigar—because I'm so grateful that teacher mixed up our kids all those years ago so you could be in my life. And because I can text you nothing but a poop emoji and you know exactly what I mean. And because you (and sometimes Noor) can get me unstuck when I need it.

The kids in my life—because I started reading the lovely books from my childhood again when you told me to. And because Omar is Ahmed and Ayesha is Sara, and without planning it, Adam ended up on the cover. And because Hana is the only one I can share favorite books and characters with, and because Sofie loves me enough to fill up my water bottle despite the ladybugs.

Muna—because of the way you always know how to show up when I need it the most—whether in person, via care packages of Turkish Delight, or cards with Inigo Montoya on the cover, filled with beautiful words I've kept close and safe and refer back to often. And because you married Khurshid, who tolerates our cackling late into the night and still makes us scrambled eggs in the morning.

Minoo—because of all the Punjabi dances, literal and figurative, across decades and oceans and through all the times I've needed it. There have been so many. And because at the end of the day it's you and me on the couch.

And finally, to my parents. Because everything.